WITHOUT A WORD, I DRESSED...

My hands were shaking. I felt light-headed with lust. This was not good.

"Ready," I said with an unsteady voice.

Once again, Rook avoided eye contact, but swooped me into his arms.

I needed to say something. Something that would make him believe I was here to work and meant it.

"I'm sorry you had to see me like this." I stared at his face—that strong jaw inked with black stubble, the elegant curve of high cheekbone.

"I am not. I quite enjoyed it."

What? "Why do you keep toying with me like that, Rook? Is this some game to you?"

He stopped in the soft white sand, clutching me in his arms as if I weighed nothing. "My apologies. You are right. I drew the line. I should maintain it."

"Drawing a line. Is that what you call it?"

He looked at me with furrowed dark brows.

"You're the master of the mind fuck, Rook. You say make yourself at home, you say you want to help, but..." I pulled myself back. I was losing control again.

OTHER WORKS BY MIMI JEAN PAMFILOFF

COMING SOON!
The Goddess of Forgetfulness (Book 4, Immortal Matchmakers, Inc. Series)
Skinny Pants (Book 3, The Happy Pants Café Series)
Check (Part 3, Mr. Rook's Island Series)
Digging A Hole (Book 3, The Ohellno Series)

THE ACCIDENTALLY YOURS SERIES
(Paranormal Romance/Humor)
Accidentally in Love with…a God? (Book 1)
Accidentally Married to…a Vampire? (Book 2)
Sun God Seeks…Surrogate? (Book 3)
Accidentally…Evil? (a Novella) (Book 3.5)
Vampires Need Not…Apply? (Book 4)
Accidentally…Cimil? (a Novella) (Book 4.5)
Accidentally…Over? (Series Finale) (Book 5)

THE FATE BOOK SERIES
(Standalones/New Adult Suspense/Humor)
Fate Book
Fate Book Two

THE FUGLY SERIES
(Standalones/Contemporary Romance)
fugly
it's a fugly life

THE HAPPY PANTS SERIES
(Standalones/Romantic Comedy)
The Happy Pants Café (Prequel)
Tailored for Trouble (Book 1)
Leather Pants (Book 2)
Skinny Pants (Book 3) SPRING 2018

IMMORTAL MATCHMAKERS, INC., SERIES
(Standalones/Paranormal/Humor)
The Immortal Matchmakers (Book 1)
Tommaso (Book 2)
God of Wine (Book 3)
The Goddess of Forgetfulness (Book 4) WINTER 2017

THE KING SERIES
(Dark Fantasy)
King's (Book 1)
King for a Day (Book 2)
King of Me (Book 3)
Mack (Book 4)
Ten Club (Series Finale, Book 5)

THE MERMEN TRILOGY
(Dark Fantasy)
Mermen (Book 1)
MerMadmen (Book 2)
MerCiless (Book 3)

MR. ROOK'S ISLAND SERIES
(Romantic Suspense)
Mr. Rook (Part 1)
Pawn (Part 2)
Check (Part 3) COMING 2018

THE OHELLNO SERIES
(Standalones/New Adult/Romantic Comedy)
Smart Tass (Book 1)
Oh Henry (Book 2)
Digging A Hole (Book 3) COMING 2018

PAWN

Mr. Rook's Island
Part Two

Mimi Jean Pamfiloff

A Mimi Boutique Novel

PAWN

PROLOGUE

It wasn't supposed to be like this, you know. Such a fucking mess. But I should've guessed this was coming. Because when life becomes nothing but should-haves, there is no other possible outcome. My big sister, Cici, *should've* come home from her exotic island vacation four months ago. My father *should've* told me that Mr. Rook, the owner of the resort, came to see him with the news that Cici had drowned, instead of leaving me in the dark. I *should've* known better than to borrow money from a very dangerous man in order to fund my search for her. There are so many should-haves that I'm sick to my stomach with remorse.

But by far, my biggest regret is the moment I stepped foot on this island. Because once I set eyes on the devastatingly handsome Mr. Rook, I couldn't stop myself from wanting him, from dreaming about him, from feeling drawn to the connection between us. I know it's wrong.

Nothing good will come of it.

Because now I'm beginning to believe that Cici didn't die drunk, swimming in the middle of the night. Just like I suspect that this past week with Rook—the touches, the forbidden kisses, the sexual hunger in his steel blue eyes—was an elaborate hoax meant to distract me.

Because he's not just a wealthy businessman.

This island is no paradise.

And I'm no fucking idiot.

So while resisting this man will be the hardest thing I've ever done, I *will* find out what really happened to my sweet Cici. Otherwise I won't ever be able to let her go, and my broken heart will be the end of me.

My name is Stephanie Fitzgerald. I am twenty-six years old, London born, New York raised, and I am the newest employee of Mr. Rook's Island, where "your fantasy is our business."

CHAPTER ONE

"Miss Fitzgerald, please see me in my private office after the meeting," Mr. Rook growled as he blew into the conference room like an angry storm.

My stomach curdled. It was my first day on the job, and while I hadn't expected him to be overjoyed by my presence, the outright hostility was a surprise. *At least, this early in the game.*

"For?" I asked, masking my uneasiness in front of the strange faces around the long gray table. I could only assume the resentful stares belonged to Rook's senior staff, though I'd only arrived thirty seconds before him, and we'd all yet to be introduced.

And I see we're off to a great start. These people would be reporting to me—the woman who'd been just another guest last week.

And exactly why had I asked for the executive manager's job at the end of my trip? Simple. I needed a reason to stay. I needed to be in a position of trust. I needed to find answers, something I wouldn't be getting from the beautiful conniving man who'd built this exclusive resort, where their claim to fame was that they could make any woman's fantasy come to life. From what I'd seen, that part was true, though most guests just wanted to romp with a male character from the latest movies—Mr. Grey, Aquaman, Thor—or the timeless heroes born to the classics like Darcy, Tarzan, or Captain Hook. And for a hefty price, ranging from fifty thousand to a million bucks, Rook's Island could deliver. They had every set and prop imaginable to create the ultimate fantasy vacation experience, including submarines, a pirate ship, and a Scottish castle. I'd even heard they had a cityscape—for the CEO/billionaire fantasies—and a cattle ranch complete with a hot cowboy who gave naked riding lessons.

Different strokes, I suppose.

But what interested me most wasn't the hot men or the exotic sex. It was the stuff Rook kept hidden. I'd witnessed enough to know that there was way more to this place than he'd let on, and I guessed those secrets had something to do with Cici's death.

How or why?

Not sure. But Mr. Rook, the master of illusions, had gone to great lengths last week to distract me, to make me believe that Cici's death was accidental. He'd soothed my grief over the loss of a sister who'd been more like a mother. He'd held me and told me how sorry he was for not preventing it. He almost made love to me.

I won't be played again.

"Miss Fitzgerald, are we interrupting your day-dreaming?" Rook snarled in his neatly pressed, black linen suit, gray button-down shirt, and pale blue tie that matched his nearly translucent eyes. The stunning bastard of a man wore his costume well.

Sitting across from him at the head of the table, I forced my gaze to his angry, handsome face and tried not to lose my shit on the first day.

I cleared my throat and forced a smile on my face. "Yes, of course, Mr. Rook. I will come see you after the meeting."

He gave a curt nod with his head of thick dark hair. "And since you have managed to steal the attention of my staff, why don't you introduce yourself—not that we don't already know who you are."

With my hair pulled into a ponytail and dressed in my last clean outfit, a lavender T-shirt and denim short-shorts, I stood from my chair. "Hi, everyone," my voice squeaked.

Wow. Nice. While I would generally describe myself as average—average confidence, average wavy brown hair and brown eyes, and average five-four height—I felt like an above average moron for thinking I could pull this off. I didn't belong here. Not as a guest and certainly not as an employee. They had to see that.

Despite my fear of everyone catching on, I raised my chin. "I'm Stephanie Fitzgerald. Obviously, you're all aware that I was a guest last week, thus my informal outfit. Fortunately, however, I'll be wearing a uniform soon, since Mr. Rook has generously offered me the position of executive manager." As I said those words, I realized that the seated people around the table, save Rook, might've had their sights on the role after Mrs. Day, the prior manager, had been fired.

That explains the hostility.

"And why don't you share your background with us, Stephanie? Tell us what made you want to take on such a demanding position." Rook's tone oozed of condescension like he wanted to make a fool of me.

Of course he does. Like the staff, he didn't want me here. Likely because he knew I couldn't care less about his fucking paradise, nor did I buy his story about Cici. She had been far too responsible to get drunk and take off for a night swim in the ocean like Rook said. He'd only agreed to give me the job because he'd promised to do "anything" to help me move past my sister's tragic death and get my life back on track.

My gaze traveled over the expectant faces around the table, all twenty-something men and women of a variety of ethnicities—black, white, Latino, and Asian. Rook had a very diversified crew, which made sense. They served anyone with money—okay, any woman with money—and that meant they needed to cater to a variety of clients, albeit primarily Americans from what I'd seen. My guess was that he limited his exposure this way. His customers only came from countries where he had influence. Influence to keep his island a secret.

Not for long.

"I think what you're all really wondering is what makes me qualified to help run this resort. Great question." Still standing, I planted my hands on the table like I owned the damned place. They had to believe I belonged. "I've just spent one week sampling the food, interacting with the staff, and observing the engagement processes with the guests. I'm not going to lie, everyone here does an impeccable job—the attention to detail, the welcoming atmosphere, and the quality of the experiences you provide. But I did see room for improvement, and it should be every business's primary goal to pursue perfection. *That*, my friends, takes a set of fresh eyes."

"So you think you're qualified because you can point out all of the things they've done wrong?" Rook asked with a sadistic smirk on his lips.

Poke away, jerk. You're not going to rattle my cage. I wasn't leaving this dump until I got what I came for. The truth. Possibly revenge. *No, definitely revenge.*

"Mr. Rook," I chuckled sweetly, "I would never diminish the hard work these people obviously put in to running your resort. I am simply saying that I can help take *great* to the next level, even though I am sure I have a lot to learn about how things are done around here. For example, who is responsible for the husband harem?" I looked around the table, and a woman with short blonde hair and a thin frame, likely in her mid-thirties, raised her hand. She wore a blue and white Hawaiian-style shirt, as did all of the employees on the island. I assumed I'd soon be getting my own fancy uniform, too.

"I'm in charge of the harem," she said with a bite.

"And what's your name?" I asked.

"Linda?" she replied.

No, it wasn't a question. But I could tell by her tone that she expected me to ridicule her, though I had no intention of making enemies of the staff. I needed them to trust and like me. I needed them to tell me everything they knew about this place and its owner.

"Great. Linda," I said, "I'm sure you are aware that I was mistakenly brought to the harem last week." The husband harem was this enormous extravagant tent filled with stunningly hot, naked men who had sex with the guest of honor. I had been brought there by mistake when one of the new employees mixed me up with another guest.

"Yes, I heard," she said, shifting in her leather exec chair.

"Well, it was an honest mistake," I said. "But it was one that gave me an opportunity to see what an incredible job you do controlling quality. I mean, wow." I fanned my face. "There wasn't one man in that harem who wasn't a specimen of male perfection." They were ripped, tan, and hung—perfect tens. Of course, no man compared to Rook. The perfect lines of his strong jaw, the sensual lips, the tall lean muscular body with broad shoulders. His thick dark hair and stunningly pale eyes made him seem more like a Greek god rather than a mere mortal who owned an island of dark secrets.

Linda's expression lightened. "That's why the harem is our favorite fantasy. The tent is booked every operationally active day of the year."

"And that's my point. We need another one. It's just that good. And clearly the guests love it, so I assume we're turning away requests. I'd like to see a plan from you to add a second tent, including timing for staffing." I had to believe that finding the right kind of men wouldn't happen overnight. Those guys—or fantasy hosts, as they were called here—were like a collection of fine wines that could only be acquired over time with the utmost care.

I smiled at Linda and could tell by the proud flicker in her brown eyes that I'd won her over. *One down.*

"As for what else qualifies me," I said, "I have a master's in international relations from NYU, and have worked at the New York City Chamber of Commerce for the past three years. I can bring perspectives on emerging cultural trends as well as insights about the categories of businesses flourishing globally.

"The world is shrinking," I planted my index finger onto the table, "and for this island to keep up, we'll need to look ahead. We should be tapping into other markets and diversifying our fantasy offerings. We need to know which economies are growing fastest and have women with the most disposable income. China, for example. What do their wealthiest women want? Emperors? Dragons? Both? We should start—"

"All great points, Miss Fitzgerald," Rook cut in with a snarl, "but this is my island. I decide who we market to and what fantasies we offer."

Still nervous as hell on the inside, I arched a brow and offered Rook a bitchy little smirk, not breaking character. "Then I guess I'll have to get you alone in a room and bring you around to my way of thinking. How's after this meeting?"

Rook's eyes sizzled with anger. Evidently, he didn't appreciate the fact that his efforts to intimidate me weren't working. Or maybe it was the sexual undertone of my comment and the fact I was acting like his boss.

Good. I'm here to fuck with your head, Rook. Every minute of every day until I got what I wanted. Luckily, I'd spent this last week learning from the pro. Him.

"Take a seat, Miss Fitzg—"

"Stephanie. Call me Stephanie. I don't care for formality. It's old-fashioned and doesn't foster candid conversations, which is something I expect from all of you."

The expressions around the table were a mixture of smirks and "oh boy, this is gonna get ugly."

Rook cleared his throat. "Formality and rules are what maintain standards of quality, Miss Fitzgerald. I suggest you get used to it."

I took my seat, neatly folded my hands on the table, and prepared to poke the bear with a hot branding iron.

"I am all too familiar with your *rules*." I scoffed. "But I assumed after last week, they had some room for bending."

Rook's face visibly heated to the precipice of outright rage—flat lips, red cheeks beneath his thick dark stubble, and a slight flare to his perfect nostrils on his perfect fucking nose.

Oh no. Did "Miss Fitzgerald" cross the line?

As for the "rule," he knew exactly what I meant. It was the one about keeping his glorious dick in his tailored linen pants. Because he wasn't just the owner of the island. Oh no, not even close. And his secret was the kind of bizarre, unbelievable bullcrap I had yet to digest because it made no sense and never would. According to him, the man sitting before me in his fine suit was a façade created for the sole purpose of protecting this island from the outside world with a fortress of cash. According to him, this was sacred ground. As for why he'd been burdened with the responsibility of being its caretaker, well, that was one more unbelievable morsel. This island used to be home to a group of monks, and he was the last.

No, that wasn't a fucking joke. *You just can't make this stuff up.* The callous, well-dressed man sitting before us was a monk.

How he came up with the idea of having a resort that provided sexual fantasies to women, I couldn't understand. Religious people didn't run brothels—not that this island was a whorehouse, but, at the end of the day, the principles were the same. Women came here for pleasure, albeit expensive and packaged as an elaborate "fantasy getaway," but it wasn't the sort of thing a monk or church would condone. Regardless, Rook still had his "rules," and that meant no sex. Not ever. Yet it hadn't stopped him from trying last week. Luckily, we were interrupted. *And I'll never let him touch me again.*

I'd come to my senses since then.

Rook's expression relaxed, like he'd willed himself to gain control. "You're mistaken, Miss Fitzgerald. My rules are for obeying and so am I. Which is something you and I will discuss after the meeting." He turned his attention to the room, effectively shutting me down. "Now, as for the topics we need to discuss…"

Rook went on about the cleanup efforts on the island and asked each person to give updates on their particular areas of responsibility. A hurricane had rolled through two days ago, and they'd had to evacuate the guests—I stayed behind, of course. Anyway, the rain and winds had moved on yesterday, and now everyone was working to restore services, make repairs, and restock any supplies that had been ruined. All in all, however, Rook had made this place hurricane proof.

An hour later, Rook began wrapping up. "Obviously, we are in no state to welcome guests this week, but please plan on having a full planeload next Monday. Stephanie will be shadowing each of you, learning the ropes. I will be at your disposal if you need anything." Rook rose from his chair. "That'll be all."

The employees stood and shuffled from the room, busily jotting on notepads or chatting on their walkie-talkies.

I remained seated, mentally preparing myself for battle.

"Ready for that meeting?" I said cheerfully.

Rook waited for the room to empty. Once it did, he drew a slow, chilling breath that made the hairs stand up on the back of my neck, all of them waving little black flags. "I don't know what game you're playing, Stephanie, but I assure you, it won't be tolerated."

So we're using first names again now that we're alone, huh?

I leaned back in my chair, crossed my arms, and hunkered down. He couldn't see me sweat. I had to convince him I was here to do my job and do it well.

"Oh, now, James. You agreed to hire me, knowing full well what you were getting. So don't tell me you're thinking of backing out of our agreement or that you're intimidated by a strong woman." I tsked. "I thought you were the secure type."

He let out a venomous laugh. "I've yet to meet a secure man who tolerates blatant insubordination."

"I was only making suggestions, James. A girl is entitled to her opinion, isn't she?"

"You are no girl. And you are entitled to nothing. Not on my island. These are my employees and you will—"

I jerked to my feet and slapped my hands on the table. "I will remind you that my sister died on your island due to your negligence. I will remind you that I'm here because you offered—no, you begged—to help me move on. Well, this is me, Rook, moving on. So if that costs a few bruises to your precious ego, then so fucking be it. But don't ever belittle me, or try to make me look stupid for having an opinion."

His large body tensed, and I was sure that if I'd been standing next to him, he'd be dragging me out of the room by my hair for a good old-fashioned flogging. No, not a joke. That was how I'd found out about him being a monk. I'd caught him in the jungle, naked in the rain, beating the hell out of his back as penance for almost fucking me. The man was old school when it came to punishments.

"I will do as I please, Miss Fitzgerald," he said in a menacingly low tone. "If it does not suit you, you may—"

"Will you really? Do as you *please*? Because last I remember, you couldn't work up the nerve. Then you left me hanging." I tilted my head to the side, beginning to feel genuinely riled up as memories of that night filled my head. The heat of his skin against mine. His hands on my bare breasts. The head of his thick cock nudging at my entra—

Jesus, Steph. Clearly, I was losing control. And from the way his stubbled jaw flexed and those icy blue-gray eyes narrowed on my lips, I was sure his anger was being replaced by something else, too.

Crap. Get a hold of yourself. I would accomplish nothing if I started falling for him again. Or got kicked off the island prematurely. But this was a sticky game I was playing: pushing Rook to trust me. He had to see that I was just as fierce as he was when it came to protecting this island. He had to believe that I would fight for what was best, even if it pissed him off. There was no other way.

I sat slowly and turned on the demure Stephanie. "Sorry. I didn't mean that," I said with fake remorse, staring at the table. "I know you have...a unique set of circumstances. And that you weren't cruel to me on purpose."

Really, I didn't *know* anything aside from the fact that he'd used every trick in the book to distract me last week so I wouldn't dig into Cici's death. I guessed he also didn't want me to notice all of the strange things going on in the place. But now that I thought about it, even the guest check-in process was a red flag. They actually took saliva samples upon arrival, telling us it was an STD test—"merely a precaution." I'd bought it. Now I didn't. Saliva swabs were normally for DNA tests.

But why?

I looked at Rook from across the room, where he remained standing and keeping his distance. I wondered if it was because I'd pissed him off or because his lust for me hadn't entirely been an act. Penises don't lie, and his had been ready.

I continued with my performance. "I don't know if it's because this island is where Cici died and being here makes me feel close to her again, but I feel a special connection with this place. I want to stay here—I *need* to stay here—but I'd also like for you to be happy with my work, James. That said, if you don't want me here, then put me on the first plane home." Of course, there was no way in hell I'd be leaving. I banked on the fact that he suspected I knew more than I'd let on and that letting me loose in the world wouldn't serve to keep his island a secret from the masses.

His eyes stuck to my lips for a long, conspicuous moment before snapping back to meet my gaze. "If you do not change your attitude, I won't hesitate." He walked past me, pausing in the doorway. "And you will refer to me as Mr. Rook."

Whatever floats your lying-ass boat. "Okay, *Mr. Rook.*"

"I need to take care of something. I will send for you when I'm ready for our talk. In the meantime, I suggest you find a way to make yourself useful. We have guests arriving in a week."

He left the room, and I collapsed on the inside, my nerves hammering at the walls of my sour stomach. *Fucking hell. How am I going to get through this?* I planned to ruin this man for whatever he'd done to my poor sister, but being in the same room with Rook made me lose my mind.

Of course, maybe I wasn't the only one suffering from unwanted emotions. Rook had just bailed on our little meeting and fled the room to "take care of something." I wondered if that something was between his legs.

Suddenly, the image of him doing just that invaded my mind—his head thrown back in ecstasy, his large hand wrapped around his thick shaft, stroking vigorously. A wave of unwelcome pulses shot between my legs.

"Crap." I let out a long, calming breath and scrubbed my hands over my face. I'd have to work fast and get the hell out of here. Because staying in control around Rook was going to be harder than I'd thought.

CHAPTER TWO

After I cleared the storm of uninvited feelings from my mind, I left the conference room and made my way to the main office space just down the hall, where they had a pool of twenty cubicles occupied by a small army of people.

As I had learned last week from Rook, the operators handled everything from room-service orders and excursion requests to maintenance and fantasy schedule changes. Today, there were no guests, so I assumed everyone was busy with hurricane cleanup, like making sure the island's immaculate gardens and gravel walkways were cleared of debris or ensuring all of the underground structures weren't flooded. I hadn't seen much of the operation's guts, except for this particular office situated beneath Rook's mansion, but we were in hurricane alley. With reason, much of the infrastructure had been built below ground and came equipped with industrial generators that pumped away any water that snuck into stairwells or openings. My guess was that building down instead of up also preserved the lush jungle and natural landscape.

Anyway, my first task at hand was to get the lay of the land. Second, I needed to find out where Rook stashed important information, such as contacts he bribed to keep this island hidden from the world, bank records, and most importantly, the guest lists. If my suspicions were correct, Cici wasn't the first person to go missing, and I wasn't the first person to come looking for a loved one. Rook had to keep records of that and anything else he might see as a threat. Finally, I wanted to find out more about the women who'd been wearing red butterfly pendants last week. There had been five. All elderly, all of them supposedly VIP guests who received the best fantasy a million dollars could buy. But Rook had lied to me about the details of their vacations— that they'd come for some sort of loved-one reenactment fantasy. Then, as we were evacuating three days ago, I saw five young women wearing the same red butterfly pendants. Call me crazy, but they looked like those old ladies. Only, they weren't elderly. They looked twenty at best.

People just don't lose sixty years off their faces and bodies. But I'd also seen Rook's hair go salt and pepper in a day, then turn midnight black the next. Was it my imagination that his skin had looked younger, too? Or had he just made a quick visit to the Just for Men aisle and my mind let me see what it wanted? I didn't know, but I was here to find out.

As I stood at the back of the cubicles, watching the staff on their headsets and typing away on their computers, I listened in on the woman closest to me, taking notes for maintenance requests—"North dock. Repair needed. Got it. Yacht from slip number thirty has taken on water. Got it. Power down at harbor master's station..." It dawned on me that this wasn't their first hurricane and it wouldn't be their last. They had a process, and I wouldn't be of much help by simply standing here.

Not going to learn anything either.

"Stephanie!" a deep voice called out.

I turned my head to find Luke, the scuba instructor, standing in a damp white T-shirt and cutoff jeans. I'd met him a little over a week ago on welcome night. He was tall, tan, and extremely handsome. He'd also made his interest in me known.

That means he's an ally.

"Luke!" I went to my tiptoes and gave him a hug. He smelled like fresh sweat and seawater.

Luke released me and beamed down with his hazel eyes. "I just heard the good news, boss. Does this mean I get a raise now that you're in charge?"

I play slapped his arm. "Absolutely. How's an extra million a year?"

"Great! But I'd really hoped to get a company car, too." He smirked, and I laughed. There was nowhere on this island to drive anything but a golf cart.

"I've got a brand-new fully loaded Jeep waiting right outside for you."

He made a sour face. "I had to drive those in the

military. Not a fan."

"Oh, sorry." I leaned in. "I forgot about your past life." He'd told me last week that he'd served in the marines for several years and came to the island to find peace and quiet. I got the impression that he'd been through a lot.

"No problem." His lips curled into a sneaky little smile. "I'll forgive you if you have dinner with me tonight."

"Oh, I really..." I hit pause on my rejection. Last week, Rook had nearly pummeled Luke for hitting on me. Then Rook and I almost had sex, and after that, Rook made it clear he would have to steer clear of me for the remainder of my stay. I was too much temptation. Which was why, when I'd demanded a job, I'd assured him that I fully respected his beliefs and would keep things professional between us. After all, what sort of sadistic woman pursued a man who'd taken a vow of chastity and was completely unavailable? Yes, Rook was sexier than hell and had kissed me like—

Stop. Just stop. He can't be trusted.

Things were different this week. This week, I needed Rook to let his guard down and trust me—I wasn't here to seduce him or prove he was a liar. I was here to work.

"Yes. Dinner sounds great." I leaned in. "As long as I'm not breaking any rules? No one's given me the employee handbook just yet."

Luke's clean-shaven face glowed. "I can assure you that employee fraternization is strongly encouraged here on the island." He winked. "We're all adults. And adults need company."

Of course. Why wouldn't the rules be different? We weren't working for just any old company. This was the island of indulgences—sex, drinking, eating, exploring your wildest fantasies.

"In that case," I said, "I'll have dinner with you on one condition."

He cocked one light brown brow in question.

"Everyone's busy with the hurricane cleanup," I said, "and I don't want to bother them. Can you show me around?"

"Actually, that's why I'm here. Rook asked me to help you settle in to your new staff quarters."

"Really?" I masked my shock. Rook was obviously making a statement, somewhere in the realm of "fuck you." Because last week, despite being tied to a vow of chastity, Rook had made it clear he didn't want to see me with another man. *"I may be a monk, but I'm no saint. You know I want you."*

Okay. This is actually good. It meant Rook took my employment seriously. He couldn't run around acting like a jealous boyfriend.

"Really." Luke nodded. "Rook pulled me off salvage duty just to come find you—we lost two yachts in the storm."

"Well, lucky me. I can't wait to see my new home."

Luke flashed a suspiciously wolfish grin. "And I can't wait to show you."

CHAPTER THREE

"Roommates?" I swiveled toward Luke, who stood in the doorway of a rather nice-sized, two-bedroom apartment situated in an underground complex. It had a modern open kitchen and cozy living room with a deep khaki armchair and couch, and a sixty-inch flat screen. A tropical fish tank, teaming with little neons and built into the wall, gave the room a natural feel despite the lack of sunlight.

Okay, it's nice. So what? I can't live with Luke. The bigger question was why would Rook want me to?

"This is a joke, right?" I asked.

Luke crossed his toned arms over his chest. "Wow. Can't say I've ever felt this flattered."

"No. Sorry. It's not about you. It's just," I toggled my finger between us, "you're a man. I'm a woman. We can't—"

"We can't share an apartment because it would be too indecent and your mother might object?"

Ohmygod. Ohmygod. What did this mean? Rook had made a huge statement by sending Luke to help me settle in. But making him my roomie? This was a complete dismissal, Rook's way of saying I had zero importance to him. I couldn't lie, it stung a little even if I knew my attraction for him wasn't right. Or smart.

Careful, Steph. Rook might be watching us. He had a control room where he monitored almost every space on the island, including the fantasies as they played out. He claimed it was for safety and quality control. *And watching you squirm while he fucks with your head.*

"Stephanie, you look a little pale. You okay?" Luke gripped me by the shoulders.

"Yeah. I'm fine." I couldn't let Rook know he'd gotten to me. This could be a test. *But to prove what?*

I mentally scrambled. "Sorry. It's just when you mentioned my mother might object…" I drew a deep breath for dramatic effect. "My mother is dead. And I lost my sister recently, too. I think it still shocks me sometimes, you know?"

Luke's tanned face turned pasty, and he dropped his hands. "I'm sorry. I didn't know."

"How could you? We hardly know each other." I looked at the polished travertine floor.

Luke reached out and lifted my chin. "I think I'm finally beginning to understand."

"Understand what?" I blinked.

"Why you always have that pained look in your eyes. But you don't need to hide it around me. I've been through the emotional grinder and I get it.

You can always talk to me."

"Thanks. But please don't worry about me." I offered Luke a comforting smile. "Other than ensuring you lift the seat, flush, and wash your own dishes, of course."

"I'm a forty-two-year-old man and set in my ways, Stephanie." A sly grin lifted the corners of his lips. "The toilet-seat thing is asking a lot."

I laughed and lightly socked his shoulder. "Whatever, roomie."

"Ow!" He cupped his strong hand over his fake wound. "You punch hard."

"Don't you forget it."

Suddenly, Luke's hazel eyes floated down to my lips, and I froze. I hadn't had time to mentally regroup and think about my strategy now that Rook had thrown me this curveball. Should I let Luke kiss me? But then what if he wanted that to lead to more? Luke was an attractive man—a solid eleven on a scale of one to ten—but I was only here for one thing, and every move I made had to bring me closer to my goal. Plus the clock was ticking on my "loan" from Warner Price. He was not a nice man, but he'd been the only option to finance the cost of my vacation. In exchange, I had agreed to do some work for him related to the island.

On that note…

I stepped back from Luke and glanced at my bedroom doorway. "Well, I guess I'll check out the accommodations and get my things unpacked. By the way, where can I make a phone call? I need to check in with a few people."

"There's a small media room at the end of the hallway outside. You can check personal emails and Skype or call home. Just remember not to mention the island to your friends and family." He leaned in to whisper, "I think Rook listens in on phone calls."

That's not at all intrusive. It would make having a conversation with Warner Price a little difficult.

"I understand," I said. "Gotta keep this place a secret." They all claimed it was about protecting their clientele's privacy, but I suspected there were bigger reasons for staying off the grid.

"Great," said Luke. "I'll be back in an hour to give you that tour. I'm sure as the island's new manager, you'll want to see how the cleanup and repairs are coming along."

"Sounds good. Oh, and thanks, Luke. For everything."

"No. Thank you for joining our little family. I think you'll be good for the island. And you'll be great for me." He left me there to ponder that little nugget. Maybe he expected our living situation to result in something more. *Maybe he's been assigned to poison my coffee in exchange for a promotion.* At this point, anything was possible.

The moment Warner Price heard my voice on the

other end of the phone, an ominous growl erupted in my ear.

Great. He's pissed, too. Like Rook, he was not the sort of man anyone wanted to make angry, least of all me.

"Well, I'm fucking waiting, Stephanie. Where the hell are—"

"Sir," unsure who might be listening, I cut in before he might say anything to undermine my act, "I am so sorry I haven't called sooner, but before you *say* anything, you need to know that I just now *listened* to your voicemails."

Warner Price hadn't left me any voicemails—he wasn't the message-leaving sort—so I hoped he would catch on.

I continued, already feeling the air run thin in this tiny gray closet deemed the staff media room. "Let me say I feel honored that you're so insistent about offering me that job to come work for you." I'd already agreed to work for him, but this wasn't your standard employee-employer relationship.

After Cici had gone missing, it had been nearly impossible to find any contact information for this place since they demanded complete confidentiality from the guests and controlled all access to and from the resort via private planes. It had taken me three months just to get a web address with a very nondescript reservation request/questionnaire. Somehow, they'd approved me, but then came the next hurdle. I had to prepay for the trip immediately or lose my spot. Banks simply didn't loan money for this sort of stuff, so I found Warner Price, a man who likely belonged to the mob or something equally shady. Desperate to find my sister, I told him about Rook's resort, a place somewhere near the Bermuda Triangle. Okay, actually that had been a guess. I didn't know where the island was, and I still didn't. It was so private no country claimed it, and it wasn't on any maps—not formally. Warner hadn't found that remotely interesting until I explained the part about my sister going missing and that no one, not the US or Bahaman government, would get involved. Add to that the large sums of money flowing through the resort, and it made for a perfect investment for a guy like Warner, who likely found the money-laundering potential exciting. Plus, no government meant no laws could be broken. There weren't any. So Warner agreed to give me the money to get to the island and find my sister, under two conditions:

One, I had to become part of his team. He claimed that if everything worked out, he couldn't have me running around, knowing about a key piece of his operation—whatever the hell that was.

Two, I had to bring back very specific information about Rook: where he was from, what other properties or businesses he owned, who he bribed to keep his island a secret, and so on. Basically, Warner needed to know who he was up against and who he'd have to keep happy once he took over the resort.

Obviously, I'd agreed to all his demands.

I went on, attempting to make sure Warner knew we might not be alone on the phone line. "Anyway, I'm calling to say that while I am very much interested in your offer—I mean the job sounds *tough* and *time*-consuming, but very interesting—I decided to accept another offer."

"What kind of offer?" he asked.

"It's in the travel industry—managing a resort, actually. The job just sort of popped up, and it's a great opportunity to learn, so I couldn't pass it up. I hope you understand?" *And I hope you were able to read between the lines.*

"Well, then, I suppose congratulations are in order."

I whooshed out a breath of relief. He sounded firm, but no longer pissed. He got everything I'd just told him. Or not told him.

"Thank you."

"No thanks needed," he replied. "But I would like to keep in close contact. You may decide you don't like the new role and change your mind about my offer. When will you be back in town? I'll take you to lunch."

Crap. He might be speaking like Mr. Polite, but Warner was a criminal. Ruthless and wealthy. His lunch comment likely meant he wanted an exact time frame.

"I'm not sure yet," I said. "But soon."

"Don't wait too long, Stephanie, or I might start thinking you're brushing me off."

Fuck. How much time was "too long"? Weeks? A month? Warner had made it clear that he would go after my friends and family if I displeased him.

On the family side, I really only had my father, who was somewhere off in the Middle East, and I doubted he'd be hurrying back since we weren't on good terms. Honestly, we never would be again. Not after I'd learned that Rook had gone to see him and personally delivered the terrible news about Cici. But instead of my dad telling me, he'd chosen to leave me in the dark. He claimed he'd done it to protect me from the pain, but really, my father was just messed in the head. He never got over losing my mother after I was born, and years of reporting in war zones hadn't helped. Now he'd lost Cici, too, and I had to wonder if it pushed him over the edge. I mean, how could he just let me suffer like that? Though she and I were only six years apart, Cici had practically raised me. She made my lunches and patched up my skinned knees. She helped me with my homework and read me bedtime stories. I didn't really have anyone but her, and not knowing if she was dead or alive had nearly driven me insane with grief. It still was working a number on me.

As for any friends that Warner might go after, he'd done some digging on my Facebook account and already knew that two of my closest friends were Gwen and Yvette from my days at NYU.

In short, my dad wasn't safe, but he was safe from Warner. My friends were not.

Neither am I. Best case, I gave Warner everything he needed on Rook and ended up working for a dangerous criminal. Worst case, Warner would kill me.

"Well?" Warner pushed impatiently.

"Lunch sounds good," I said, my voice tight. "I'll be home in a few weeks. Unfortunately, I have a funeral service to plan."

"My condolences. Who died?"

"My sister. A swimming accident." If Rook was listening, it would be good for him to think I was making an effort to move on.

"I am very sorry to hear that. It must be a trying time for you. Of course, you know if you need anything, you merely have to ask. Death is easier to *deal with* when you have *friends* to take care of things."

That was the other part of this deal aside from the money. I had asked Warner to kill the person responsible for ending Cici's life. At the time, I had been blinded by rage. Now, I didn't want anyone to die. I just wanted justice.

"Thank you," I said. "I'll be sure to let you know."

"Call me next week so I know what day to expect you."

He wanted me to check in. "Of course. Thank you again."

"My pleasure, Stephanie. Goodbye."

I set down the phone and stared at my reflection on the black screen of the communal computer in front of me. The person staring back had kind, loving eyes and soft features. She wasn't equipped to deal with murderers and criminals. She didn't like lying and manipulating others.

Fucking hell. I tilted my head toward the ceiling, knowing I had to reach deep inside myself and find the strength to keep going. *Okay, I have two weeks before I need to make good on my deal with Warner.* Two weeks to get the truth.

Still, in my heart, I prayed there was some way out of all this and that there was a big, obvious explanation for everything. I didn't want Rook to be the deceitful man I thought him to be.

Keep praying, Stephanie, but you know things are only going to get uglier. A man like Rook didn't work this hard just to keep beautiful things hidden.

CHAPTER FOUR

I unpacked my suitcase containing a week's worth of dirty vacation clothes—cocktail dresses, strappy heels, two bikinis, shorts and tees—thankful that the employees were given uniforms, albeit unflattering ones. Imagine boxy blue-and-white Hawaiian shirts, khaki linen shorts, white socks, and white orthopedic sandals or running shoes.

I looked at myself in the full-length mirror on the back of my bedroom door. *A nerdy nod to Magnum P.I.*

A sharp knock jolted me in my fancy dry-weave socks.

"Stephanie? You ready?" said Luke's deep voice on the other side of the door.

"One sec!" I finished buttoning my blouse and grabbed the sunglasses from the new-employee welcome box that had been left at the door. It contained Rook-approved Ray-Bans, sunscreen, and deodorant—scent-free and forty-eight-hour lasting (not likely in this heat)—and an employee handbook. Best of all, there was a map. Not just the surface of the island, but of the underground structures. I'd literally opened it up and clacked my teeth, half excited and half in awe. *Four fucking floors below ground? Seriously? No wonder Rook charges so much money.* I knew zero about construction, but my guess was that they'd needed a considerable amount of concrete and steel to build anything that deep below sea level.

I opened the door. "Like my look?"

Luke raised his light brown brows. "Gorgeous. I love how it shows off your curves."

"I'm actually shaped like a cereal box, so yeah, this is great."

"I've seen your curves. Not a straight line anywhere." He looked me over again.

Hmm. Unless I determined it would benefit me in some way, I needed to move him away from the flirting. Yes, it was a ruthless way to think, but what else could I do? I had to be tough, even if it wasn't in my nature to hurt others.

"Okay, lover boy." I gave him a playful poke in his broad chest. "You can stop drooling now. Hey, speaking of seeing things, where's the laundromat? I desperately need to wash clothes."

"There's a stacked washer/dryer in the hall closet."

So fancy. "Does every employee have a nice apartment like this?"

"Pretty much. There's also a complimentary twenty-four-hour employee cafeteria right outside the elevators down one floor. But if you prefer to cook, there's a small store next to it. The food's not free, but you can place an order for just about anything you want. It's all delivered by plane once a week."

"Rook really takes care of his staff," I noted.

"The pay isn't as much as you'd get back home, of course, but Rook does go out of his way to pamper us. The only exception is that everyone shares an apartment unless you're a couple—they get a place with a single room."

With the way Luke spoke, he might have me believing that Rook was the kindest man on the planet.

"How long have you worked here, again?" I asked.

"About ten months." Luke's expression hinted at discomfort—shifting eyes, exaggerated smile. "Well, let's get to that tour."

Subject change, huh?

"Great," I replied. "I just need to get over to Rook's before noon." Rook had said he would send for me, but I wanted to go through his house one more time. I'd actually stayed in his guest room for a few days at his insistence after he told me Cici drowned. *"...best not to leave you alone given the recent events,"* he'd said. Really, it was all part of the illusion to make me think he cared. *Bullshit.* Either way, I'd checked out some of the house and found nothing, but I couldn't help hoping I'd missed something—a hidden storage room or a secret drawer where he stashed thumb drives. He had to keep bank records and guest profiles somewhere. Eerily, though, his home lacked any personal effects. Not one family photo or keepsake, like it was all just for show.

Regardless, I had to start somewhere, and I hadn't combed through Rook's private upstairs office.

Luke and I headed to the stainless steel elevators at the end of the long hallway inside the underground apartment complex. He pointed out the stairwell, vending machines and ice room, and the common areas for our floor, which was where the senior staff stayed. B-one. The newer or lower you were on the employee totem pole, the lower the floor you lived on. Sort of snooty, but I guessed they had to have some kind of system.

"So are all of the apartments co-ed?" I stepped onto the elevator.

Luke came in behind me and jabbed the ground-floor button. "If you're that caught up on traditional values, you have no business being here."

He'd taken offense.

"I wasn't implying anything about you. I promise I'm fine with it." I wasn't. In fact, my mind subconsciously kept drifting back to the topic. I couldn't help feeling a little wounded by Rook's blatant rejection. On the other hand, it only proved I'd been right. Rook's feelings for me had been a show. Ironically, I felt more angered than vindicated. Because now, that little part of me that felt something for Rook, something slightly more potent than lust, had been made a fool of.

Luke and I stepped out into a small enclosed lobby that looked like a brick storage shed from the outside. No one would ever guess a small city existed underneath the serene tropical landscape.

We hopped into a golf cart parked just outside, along a row of six of them.

"These carts are all over the island," said Luke. "Grab any one you want. The bellhops make sure they're charged up and parked near all of the main structures."

"It's all so organized." I got out my map.

"Rook is a perfectionist. He says that our time is more important than money."

I thought about that for a moment. "Yeah, I guess not a lot of people die wishing for more money."

"You're exactly right." Luke gave his head a quick bob. "So what do you want to see first?"

I studied the map and all its drawings of tiny trees and trails. Honest to God, it looked like an amusement park map with its little cartoon representations of the attractions: A small mountain with snow on top, labeled "Everest"; a building to the south labeled "City"; a dock to the south with a pirate ship; and a fort with little cannons sticking out from the top.

"Wow. How many fantasies do you have here?"

I asked.

"*We* have one hundred and thirty fantasy stations, though some are very small, like the blackout room, Grecian spa, or trampoline."

"Trampoline?"

Luke shrugged. "Some women like to bounce."

"I'll try not to spend too much time visualizing that one. And what's a blackout room?"

"Total darkness. It's popular with shy people."

"Oh." I was beginning to see that when it came to what women desired, I knew very little. "Let's start on the south end and work our way back." I stared at the map. "Is there really snow on that mountain?"

"This is Rook's Island, Stephanie. We've got everything."

"Including the impossible?" Because it had to be at least ninety degrees today. With the humidity, it felt like one hundred.

"We specialize in that," he said.

An hour and a half later, I'd seen a replica of a Scottish castle, the cattle ranch with twenty cows and two bulls, an overflowing waterfall, a baseball field, Greek amphitheater, office building—only ten stories and rather narrow, but fully equipped to house an entire crew of fake employees for an authentic office-based romance—swing set, bungie station, elaborate tree house for a Tarzan and Jane, romantic cabin in the woods, and the indoor fantasy complex containing all of their small one-room stations such as an S&M red room, classroom for the hot-for-teach fans, and the Grecian spa Luke mentioned earlier. I really couldn't remember it all. Each particular fantasy station had been meticulously built and decorated. No cheap painted backdrops or lame amusement park costumes. Everything looked authentic, right down to the color of the dirt or smell of the filtered air.

"It's pretty impressive," I said as we pulled up in the golf cart next to the stairwell that led down to the main offices situated directly beneath Rook's mansion.

"Each fantasy has a detailed specification you'll want to familiarize yourself with since you'll be in charge of ensuring every detail."

Wait. Luke was the scuba instructor. Now he was educating me about my role? *He's been assigned to train me.* One more slap in the face. Rook wanted there to be no doubt left in my mind that he couldn't be bothered with me. *Asshole.*

I swiftly pushed back on any ego-driven feelings. This was for the best. No temptation on his part meant no temptation on my part. Not that I would allow it. Not again.

Luke must've noticed my lips puckered with agitation because he said, "Oh, don't worry. Rook always has the island's manager try out the fantasies.

It's much easier to get a feel for what makes each one special."

"Ha-ha. Funny." Still seated in the cart, I turned to fully face him.

Luke wasn't smiling.

"Back up." My blood pressure dove for my ugly white socks. "You were joking, right?"

"Didn't Rook tell you all this when you asked for the job?"

"No, but that's insane. I'm not going to have sex with every guy on this island." And I found it hard to believe that the silver-haired Mrs. Day, who had been in her sixties, went on a fucking spree as part of her onboarding process.

"It wouldn't be everyone," Luke said. "We all know Rook is off-limits. And don't forget, some of the men, like myself, aren't fantasy hosts, so you wouldn't be having sex with us." He shot me a sly look. "Unless you wanted to."

Trying to digest his words, I ignored the come-on. *One hundred and thirty fantasies?* And Rook really expected me to just bang my way through each of them as part of my job?

"Steph?" Luke prodded for my attention.

"Oh. Sorry. It's just…I wasn't expecting the role to be so demanding." I gave him a knowing look. "I'm not good with strangers. Not like that." Casual sex and I weren't friends.

He bobbed his head, mulling it over. *Probably wondering why I'm really here, then.*

"Hopefully you can work something out with Rook," he patted my leg, "because he's a stickler for the rules, and I'd like you to stay. Still on for dinner tonight?"

Stickler, my ass.

"Dinner. Sure. As long as Rook doesn't throw me any more curveballs." I slid from the cart.

Luke chuckled. "Now, why would he do that? Not like he gets off on it," he said facetiously. "See you tonight."

I was getting the feeling that everything happening around me had been orchestrated, meant to evoke a particular response or test me. First Luke as my roomie. Now this.

Rook's trying to distract me again. There was no other explanation. But it wasn't going to work. Not this time.

I watched Luke drive off down the palm-tree-lined path toward the north side of the island, where the guest bungalows, restaurants, spa, and other non-fantasy-related sports activities were located—like tennis and scuba. They also had a dock filled with expensive yachts used for diving, dinner karaoke cruises, and whatnot.

I glanced over at Rook's large white plantation-style house with black steel shutters. It stood on a small embankment overlooking his private beach. When I'd stayed there these past few days, it felt more like staying in a museum rather than a home. The dark wood floors and antique furniture were polished to perfection and in impeccable condition. The state-of-the-art chef's kitchen appeared to have never been used. His bedroom contained nothing personal, except for a few suits in the walk-in closet. His nightstand held a Bible, but nothing more. Just like a hotel.

My conclusion? He didn't live there.

He probably lived in some weird-ass temple filled with floggers so he could punish himself every night for all his lusty, sinful daytime activities.

My mouth went dry, thinking of him naked, kneeling in the dirt beneath the stormy night sky. I had watched the muscles of his powerful arms and strong back working to deliver each painful blow. I remember feeling horrified by the sight of it, but more than anything, there'd been this twinge of anger in the back of my mind, telling me he had no right. No right to disfigure something that belonged to me.

But, of course, he didn't and never would.

I took the walkway through Rook's grassy garden lined with a few red and yellow flowers that had apparently survived the winds. I stepped onto the porch and knocked on the heavy wooden door.

No answer.

I knocked once more but got the same empty reply. *Time to snoop.* If I got caught, I could say I'd left something personal behind from my stay, like an earring.

I stepped inside. "Rook? Hello?"

It had only been a handful of hours since I'd been here, but the air smelled different, like lavender and pine. The floors had been mopped and shined.

Had he sent in the cleaning crew to remove any traces of me? I couldn't lie. It hurt a little to think that.

My gaze scaled the wooden staircase. Up there, he had his unlived-in bedroom, his office, and another room—the room *she* stayed in.

Who was she? He wouldn't say, but she'd been beyond pissed when she caught the two of us naked in his bed last week. Rook had then gotten dressed and went to her room, where they proceeded to fight in some dialect of French or-or…I wasn't sure.

"Hello?" I called out one last time for good measure.

Silence. Excellent. I raised my foot to take the first stair.

"Lovely outfit." Rook's voice echoed through my ears, nearly springing me out of my shoes.

"Jesus." I gasped, palming the space over my heart. "You scared me."

Wearing the same neatly pressed, black linen suit and light blue tie, Rook stood in the hallway that led to the guest rooms and a small reading den on the first floor. His tall frame, proud stature, and broad shoulders always gave him the appearance of coming from some elegant dinner party. I hated that he looked so gorgeous.

"My clothes are the latest in the Rook Island

collection. Do you like them?" I grabbed the hem of my oversized Hawaiian-style blouse and held it out.

"Everything looks nice on you, Miss Fitzgerald," he said, as if it were an irritant. "What are you doing here?"

I flapped my mouth for a moment, trying not to get caught up on his compliment. "Uh. Our meeting?"

"I said I would send for you."

Yes, well. I was hoping you wouldn't be here so I could dig around in your office. "Luke and I finished up with the tour, and I thought this might be a good time. But I'll come back later." I turned for the door.

"No. Wait. There is something I wish to show you." Rook marched past me and headed up the stairs.

I hesitated with my hand on the shiny white top of the railing. What the hell was this man up to?

"Coming, Miss Fitzgerald?" Rook growled, already halfway up.

"Yes." I followed him, having zero clue what came next. *A curveball, Stephanie. Haven't you learned by now? That's all he's capable of.*

"I haven't got all day," Rook snapped, waiting for me on the landing that served as another living room, with a built-in bookshelf, brass floor lamp, and cozy brown armchair. All antique, of course. All in pristine condition.

"What's going on?" I asked.

He jerked his head toward the doorway leading to his private office. "This is where you will work."

I blinked. "Sorry?"

"I'm afraid Mrs. Day decided to remodel her office with a hammer prior to her departure. And with the work required for the storm cleanup, there is no time to prepare another space for you."

Christ. It's like he knows my every move. And instead of blocking me, he shoved everything in my face. Almost as if to say, *"Look. Here's a map. And here's my office. I've got nothing to hide, Stephanie."*

"What about one of the small conference rooms?" I asked. There were several along the narrow corridor just outside the conference room we had been in this morning.

"Do you object to this room?"

Other than the fact that it's across the hall from your bedroom, where we almost fucked a few days ago?

"I feel I'd be more effective at my job if I were closer to the other staff members." Though, I was sure Rook preferred me to be as isolated as possible. If I were him, I'd want to contain me, too. *And keep a close eye on me.* Yet he'd taken me out of the guest room here, put me in an apartment with Luke, and then proceeded to bring me back to the same house, giving me an office.

Fuck. What was his game? Rook probably wanted to spin my head so fast, everything would be a blur.

I needed to take control. "I don't feel this is the

best place to work. I'll be disturbing the woman who lives in the room next door."

"She is no longer on the island. You will disturb no one."

What? "Why did she leave?"

He rubbed the side of his dark scruffy jaw, producing a bristly sound. "We no longer saw eye to eye regarding certain matters pertaining to the island."

"You mean that she caught us in bed and wasn't happy," I blurted out before thinking through my words.

Cool as ice, Rook dropped his hand from his jaw, and the corner of his full sinful lips curled into a smirk. "I thought you put that in the past." His eyes gravitated toward my mouth, sending a sensual chill through my body. "As good as it felt."

My lungs began pumping for extra air while memories of his large, strong body—grinding between my thighs—pummeled my mind. The taste of his soft lips, the feel of his rough jaw on my fingertips, the sweet smell of his hurried breath.

Fucking dammit. How, after everything, could I still be so susceptible to him?

"As far as I'm concerned, it never happened." I stepped back, but he moved closer, refusing to give me space.

"Are you sure about that, Stephanie?" he asked, his voice gravelly. "Because I have no intention of forgetting about it." Rook seemed hell-bent on playing a wicked game of mind fuck to keep me distracted. It was working.

I can't let it. Because anything that came from his mouth was a lie.

"I seem to remember the exact opposite," I pointed out. "You even said you couldn't see me again." Immediately following our close encounter, he had come to my room and confessed he wanted me, but it could never happen between us. His vow of celibacy wouldn't permit it.

"I think you know why I said that." He reached out and grabbed my chin, forcing me to gape into the depths of those hypnotic pale eyes.

My heart galloped. Locking gazes felt like traveling to another time, another place—somewhere warm that seeped through your skin and settled deep inside your bones.

My body began to tingle with the rush of oxygen and animalistic urges. Suddenly, I felt my body lean toward him. I never thought it possible to feel so much just from staring into a man's eyes, but when Rook looked at me like this, I was lost to him.

"Stephanie?"

I realized that Rook had released my chin and had been speaking the entire time, but I hadn't heard a word.

"Sorry. What?"

"So then you'll stay. Here." He looked around the sparsely decorated room—brown plantation shutters, cherry wood desk, and a leather exec chair.

Two TV screens, mounted to the wall, were on mute, one set to the Weather Channel, the other to MSNBC. They seemed incredibly out of place in this museum he called a home.

"Won't I be too close?" I asked, my voice coming out all raspy. I couldn't seem to breathe right.

Rook's eyes darted over to his bedroom doorway twenty feet away, across the landing. He smiled wickedly. "I don't believe in boundaries between my personal and work space."

He's doing it to me again. Stupid, Stephanie. Stupid, Stephanie. Fight back. "Then how do you manage to keep your vows of chastity, poverty, and obedience when they're at complete odds with your work?"

His smile dropped and so did his mood. "You really wish to know?"

"Yes." I took a small step back and crossed my arms, foolishly believing that a few extra inches between our bodies would help me keep my wits.

Rook bobbed his head, strolled over to the window, and then pulled open one of the dark shutters. Sunlight flooded the room as he peered at something outside in his garden. "I have no choice but to give everything to this island's existence, even if that means damning my eternal soul."

"So every sin you commit is justified, because you're prepared to pay the price. Wow. That allows you to get away with a lot." *Including killing people.* And the fact he was prepared to sacrifice his soul to protect this island was just one more reason for me to believe he was hiding something big because— let's face it—nobody would condemn themselves to rotting in hell for eternity just to protect a resort. And yes, he'd said the land and lagoon were sacred, but that just didn't feel like enough. There had to be more.

Rook closed the shutter and calmly came toward me, leaving little space between us. "I will get away with nothing," he said, bearing down on me with a harsh look. "And I get no pleasure from any of it."

"If you say so." I shrugged.

He narrowed his eyes, studying me for a long awkward moment before breaking the silence. "If you're going to be my right hand, it's more efficient to keep you close. Your office will be here. In my home. I insist."

Your home, yes. But you don't live here. What are you up to, Rook?

I offered him my most innocent, trustworthy smile. "As long as I'm not creating turbulence with your beliefs, it's perfect. Thank you." I gave him a nod and moved toward the desk. I needed air. "So where do you want to start? I'm sure there's a lot to learn." I opened the laptop sitting on the desk and suddenly felt the heat of his body behind me.

"Stephanie." He grabbed my shoulders and turned me to face him.

Lungs paralyzed, I looked up at the tall, tempting man with a tinge of anger in his eyes. My cheeks flooded with heat.

"This morning. What I wanted you to know…" He paused.

"Yes?"

He hesitated. "Never mind."

He released me and stepped back, gesturing for me to take a seat at the desk. "Shall we?"

CHAPTER FIVE

To my surprise, Rook hadn't brushed me off completely in terms of my training. He spent the next several hours reviewing the roles and responsibilities of the staff—fantasy schedulers, personal concierges, cleaning crew, kitchen staff, and excursion managers. There was a small team of maintenance staff for the guest bungalows and another crew dedicated to equipment and facilities for the fantasies. Including the bellhops and receptionists on standby twenty-four seven, there were well over one hundred staff members.

"And the actors?" I asked, looking at the screen ahead instead of to my side where Rook sat in a chair he'd grabbed from another room. It was taking every ounce of strength I had not to dwell on his unsaid words or not to obsess over the proximity of his fit, rock-hard body seated so closely. Even when he reached for the stupid mouse, I couldn't help noticing how his strong hands were capable of such delicate maneuvers. Normally, I would call myself out for ridiculously admiring a man's thick fingers, but the closer I looked, the more I watched him, the more I realized the scale of his physical perfection. No scars or wrinkles. No sun damage. It just wasn't possible for a man to be so effortlessly beautiful, solid and muscled in all the right places.

"They are not actors," he said, pulling me back to our conversation just in the nick of time. "They are called fantasy hosts."

"Fine. Hosts. How many are there, again?"

"Thousands; however, we maintain a smaller full-time team. The others come and go as needed, which is why we book guests up to a year in advance. The manager for each fantasy station is in charge of scheduling. You are in charge of reviewing their plan and ensuring everything is perfect."

"Is that why Luke said you expect me to sample the fantasies?"

Rook's back went ramrod straight in his chair. "He is mistaken. You will be doing no such thing." A vein on the side of Rook's neck popped out, visibly throbbing. His full lips flattened.

He's angry. Perhaps this could work for me in some way—throw the man off his game. Distracted people made mistakes. Mistakes that might tip his hand.

"What if I want to try out a few attractions?" I asked.

Rook's nostrils hinted at a flare. "Is it truly what you want?"

For one split second, I wondered if there was a Rook fantasy—a night between the sheets with his look-alike, perhaps.

"Did Mrs. Day sample the fantasies?" I asked to deflect his question.

"I think we've done enough for one day." He rose. "I must check on the crew's progress with the cleanup. You may stay here and familiarize yourself with the fantasy specifications. They'll come in useful next week when you do inspections."

I lifted a brow, unsure of what he meant.

"Before the guests arrive," he explained, "you will ensure everything has been properly prepared and that the hosts pass visual scrutiny."

"You mean...I need to physically look them over."

"Yes."

"Clothed?" I asked.

"No."

Oh boy. I wondered if I'd be responsible for applying the baby oil, too.

He continued, "And you must ensure our doctor has given them the green light."

"Saliva tests, huh?" It was what they did to guests, claiming it was some high-tech STD test. I'd never heard of such a thing, which led me to believe it was just another lie.

Rook gave me a strange look. "We do not do those for the staff. Blood tests and physical examination only."

"Why? The mouth swabs seem so efficient." I took note of what his face looked like when he lied, because I knew it was coming.

"Too expensive." He looked away, his gaze hardening. "See you at the staff meeting in the morning. Enjoy your evening."

So he looks away when he lies. I made a mental note. Nevertheless, my clock was ticking. I needed to start pressing him for more.

"What if I have questions?" I asked. "Where will you be?" He'd given me his home office, so that meant he had another work space. The small den downstairs might work, I supposed, but a private man such as himself wouldn't want me lurking around him and his secrets all day.

"I will be here. On the island," he replied bluntly.

In other words, "None of your damned business."

He left the room, and moments later, I heard the front door open and close. I got up from the desk and went to the window, spotting him making his way into the jungle, in the direction of his "sacred lagoon."

I had to follow.

"Hey, roomie. How'd your first day go?" Luke said from the open kitchen the moment I entered our apartment. He wore a plain white tee that accentuated his strong arms and well-formed pecs. On the lower half, he wore frayed cutoffs, long enough for a respectable man, but short enough to show off his tanned, muscular thighs. I had to admit he rocked the beach-bum look. Such a contrast to the tux he'd been wearing on welcome night when we'd met a little over a week ago. Luke, who looked to be in his forties, was about as handsome as they came, with stunning hazel eyes and a lady-killer smile. But when he'd hit on me, all I could do was compare him to Rook. Luke just didn't measure up.

"It was interesting," I replied. "Lots of details to remember."

Luke went back to stirring his boiling pot. "This place is all about the details. We call it 'The way of the Rook.'"

I plunked down in one of the wooden dining room chairs on the other side of the breakfast bar, realizing how sweaty and tired I felt. I'd run all over that goddamned jungle but found no sign of Rook. He hadn't even been at his precious lagoon. That place, by the way, had given me the monumental heebie-jeebies. The way the tall trees leaned away from the water and nothing grew around its edge said that I wasn't the only one who didn't like it.

"So did you hit the gym after?" Luke asked, likely noticing my sweaty look.

"There's a gym?"

Luke snickered. "Is there a gym? How do you think all of our hosts stay fit?"

Oh. Oh... "So you mean all of those men I've seen on the sets—"

"Fantasy stations," Luke corrected.

"Sorry. Fantasy stations. They all work out in this gym?" It might be a good place to listen in and befriend a few new people.

"Of course. It's in their contract. Minimum two hours a day with their trainer."

Wow. No wonder all of the men here are ripped.

Luke went on, "The rest of us are only required to work out for an hour."

And again, wow. It explained why even the bellhops looked like professional athletes.

"We can go after dinner if you like?" he offered.

"Honestly, I'm exhausted. I'm already thinking about a long hot shower and bed."

"All right. Then I'll wake you in the morning. We can go then."

Whatever. I just needed sleep. I couldn't remember the last time I'd enjoyed a solid eight. Mostly because this island put me on edge, but also because I'd begun having horrible nightmares since my arrival, the worst part being I'd started sleepwalking, too. Nothing like that had ever happened to me before, but I'd read on the Internet that extremely stressful situations caused some people to go through phases. *This fucking qualifies.*

"Sure. Gym in the morning sounds great," I said. "So what's for dinner? Please say carbs."

"Sorry. I'm making zero-carb pasta with marinara and a salad. It's the last of my organic arugula until they resume normal shipments."

I made a sour face. I liked fat. And meat. And sugar. Caffeine was nice, too. They'd been my major food groups during grad school while I also worked thirty-hour weeks, which was why it took me so long to graduate. My dad didn't earn all that much, so I'd been on my own to pay for most of my college. Cici had pitched in too, though as a kindergarten teacher she made very little. *She insisted anyway.*

My heart sank. *God, how I miss her.* I missed coming home to her smiling face and the home-cooked meals that she forced on me. I'd told her a thousand times I could fend for myself, but she wouldn't have it. "Just because Dad's never here and you and I are on our own," she'd say, "doesn't mean we can't act like a normal family." For her, that meant sitting down each night to a real dinner and talking. Looking back, I think those were the memories I cherished most. They were the moments that made us feel like we had a real home filled with real love. This fucking island had taken that from me.

"Thank you, Luke," I said with a deep sigh, sounding a little emotional.

"It's just spaghetti," he said.

"I know. But I still appreciate it. You're trying to make me feel at home, and I won't lie, home is something I miss." Without Cici, I felt adrift in a big messy world. I had no sense of direction or roots anymore. All I had was sadness and fear—of Warner

Price, of Rook, of my future.

Luke's hazel eyes looked up from his culinary pursuits, his smile melting away. "Well, we're happy to have you here, Stephanie. I hope someday you'll decide to make it your permanent home."

I stilled on the inside, simultaneously feeling flattered and taken aback. *He means it. He really means it.* I was beginning to wonder if our living arrangement wasn't an accident. Of course, I knew it wasn't. What I meant was that I'd thought this had all been Rook's doing. But now I wondered if Luke had a hand in getting me here, too.

With a twinge of guilt in my heart, because it wasn't in my nature to use or lie to anyone, I pushed myself to see the angles. If Luke genuinely wanted me, I could use it to my advantage perhaps.

"Thank you, Luke. That's very kind."

"No need to thank me. It's been a long time since I've had anyone to look after and it's a nice break from taking tourists to see sparkly fish."

I nodded slowly, the wheels churning inside my head. "Did Rook tell you to worry about me, or did you volunteer?"

"Rook may have asked me to keep an eye on you, but given your recent loss and your sudden decision to stay, I can understand why. He wants to make sure you're doing all right."

"It is a lot to take in," I admitted. "But I'm taking everything in stride. So. What else did Rook ask you to do?"

"Nothing," he said all too innocently, which sparked my suspicion.

"Did he tell you to sleep with me?" I knew the question would shock him, but that was the point. I wanted to see his reaction.

Luke jerked back his head. "No."

"Then why do you look so guilty?"

"Hey. Look. I'm not going to pretend I don't find you attractive. I made that perfectly clear the other night at the dinner club." I'd danced with Luke, and he propositioned me. Rook had not been happy.

Luke continued, "And I'd thought the feeling was mutual, but…"

"But what?"

"Rook didn't want me messing around with you, so I backed off."

"And now?" I pushed, hoping to get some sense of what Rook was up to.

"Rook assigned you to live with me when there were eight other vacancies."

I let that sink in. "He's given you the green light."

"If you want to keep things platonic—" Luke made a little shrug "—I won't be upset. I know things are different for you now; you work here. Not that the other employees let that get in the way."

"Mr. Rook is a very liberal boss," I muttered, while thinking through what this meant. Rook wanted to push me to Luke and the reasons were limited—he hoped I'd get distracted by another attractive man or that I might be taken off the playing field, making it easier for Rook to keep things professional between us.

Luke continued, "Mr. Rook is more of a realist. He doesn't believe in denying human nature."

"So he encourages everyone to sleep around?" I found that hard to believe.

"No. I think he means that forcing grown men and women into little boxes filled with arbitrary rules only makes them unhappy." Luke glanced down at his bubbling water. "And I think I need to drain the pasta before it overcooks."

Honestly, I couldn't get a read on Luke. Was he being genuine with me or playing a part like most of the people on this island?

I would assume he was on Rook's side and had been asked to keep a close eye on me. I would choose my words carefully around him, too.

CHAPTER SIX

That night, after a dinner filled with casual conversation about Luke's favorite tropical fish, followed by me finishing laundry while Luke worked out at the gym, I took a hot shower and crashed. The stress had been taking a toll on my twenty-six-year-old body. For four months, I hadn't slept well—my every breath haunted by thoughts of my sister. How had she died? Why would anyone want to end her life? Cici had not been just an honest-to-God good person and my sister, she'd cared for me while my bereaved father, a war correspondent, chased death on every front line of every war he could get his hands on. I think it was his way of escaping the pain of losing my mother to a sudden heart attack when I was young. Or maybe he was just crazy. Really, it didn't matter anymore. All that was in the past. Unchangeable. What I could change, however, was what would happen going forward.

I rolled over onto my side in my pitch-black bedroom, the tick-tock of the silver alarm clock on my nightstand echoing through my ears.

Sleep, Stephanie. Sleep, for fuck's sake. My new

bed and soft white linens were comfortable enough, but all I could think about was hunting for Rook's real office.

"Stephanie, come outside. We must speak." Rook's deep voice streamed from the doorway of my room.

"Whatthehell?" I catapulted upright, my tired eyes straining in the dark. "Rook?" My bedroom door was ajar now. Had I left it like that, too exhausted to notice?

In a white tank top and gray knit shorts, I hopped from bed. "Rook?" I peeked into the living room. The light had been left on over the stove, so I could see everything clearly, including Luke's bedroom door, which was closed. There was no sign of Rook, but I knew what I'd heard.

I went over to the front door and opened it, peeking out down the long hallway. There were ten other apartments on this floor, but all seemed quiet.

Am I dreaming again? I froze in the doorway. I felt awake. Completely and totally awake.

Okay. So maybe I'd dozed for a second and heard a voice. But now I really was awake, so what were my options? Go back to bed, where I'd get zero sleep now, or go do some snooping. If anyone saw me, I could always claim I just couldn't sleep— true—and that I'd decided to make the best of it by becoming more familiar with the island for the sake of my job. Also true.

I went back into my room, pulled my hair into a

ponytail, grabbed my running shoes and map, and headed out, closing the door quietly behind me. I took the elevator up, guessing that I had to hurry because I was likely being watched by security. Or maybe not. There were currently no guests on the island and Rook had everyone clearing fallen trees and inspecting structures.

I exited the small lobby and paused just outside, where the dimly lit walkways cut through the dark jungle and led to various parts of the island like the offices, the fantasy stations to the south, and the guest area to the north.

Which way?

If Rook's house didn't hold any information, then it was time to move on. I could try to find Mrs. Day's trashed office. There had to be lots of interesting things in there.

*Speaking of interesting...*I thought of Rook's dirty little control room housed in the same structure. He had cameras installed at every fantasy station, the beaches and bay, and at the pool and restaurant. I'd stumbled upon the room when I'd been down in the offices, looking for Rook last week. It had made me sick to my stomach at first, since I could see the guests getting romanced, picnicked, slapped around, and enjoying every flavor of consensual fucking imaginable. Rook had found me in the room and calmly put up with a good old-fashioned tongue-lashing before he had the chance to explain that they supervised each fantasy in real

time and that the hosts—or what I called actors—
wore earpieces so they could receive direction. The
job of ensuring the staff followed the guests' requests
to the letter had belonged to Mrs. Day and now it
would belong to me.

Not for long, I hoped.

I made my way down the dim gravel path. A
warm breeze dusted the tops of the trees, making the
moonlight form organic shapes on the ground.

Almost to the fork where the path split off to
the offices, I noticed a deep patch of worn earth
going off in another direction like a fresh game trail.

Or a Rook trail?

I couldn't afford to be timid or afraid. *Not anymore.* Without a flashlight, I stepped onto the path,
following it as best I could. But only twenty yards
in, I couldn't see jack. Not my nose. Not my hands.
I had to turn back before I got lost.

"Stephanie…" whispered a deep voice.

I instinctively froze. A flicker of light that appeared to be a flashlight caught my eye. *Fuck. Or it's
a lamp.*

It's hard to explain the sensation of being in a
dream, and knowing it, while a part of you fights to
stay right where it is. It wants you to keep dreaming.
That was how it had been last week when I'd
literally sleepwalked across the entire island, following a monk with a lantern. I woke to Rook shaking
me by the shoulders right as I was about to take a
swim in his sacred lagoon. Tonight felt different.

There wasn't one tiny crumb in my mind that knew this was a dream, and my nervous stomach told me to go back. Whatever was out here was darker than the night.

Fuck it.

I followed the faint light through the jungle, my feet crunching over twigs or squishing into the wet, rain-soaked dirt. After what seemed like a half hour, me ten steps away from losing my nerve and the light no longer anywhere to be seen, I spotted one of those utility sheds. The same kind covering the lobby to the staff housing and the offices.

I approached slowly and reached for the door.

"What the hell are you doing here?" said a deep familiar voice, blasting hot air into my ear.

I yelped despite knowing it was Rook.

His strong arms wrapped around me, pulling me back from the door I still faced.

"I asked you a question, Stephanie," he growled into my ear.

Shit. Shit. "I was just taking a walk."

"At two in the fucking morning?"

"I couldn't sleep," I whispered, squirming in his iron grip.

He released me, but only to turn my body toward him. "Do not lie to me, Stephanie."

It was too dark to see the fine features of his exquisite face, but I didn't have to know he was pissed as hell.

"It's not a lie. I couldn't sleep. And here I am to

prove it."

He slammed his fist past my head into the door behind me. "Bullshit! What the hell are you doing here?"

I held up my hands defensively. "I'm just going for a walk. Okay?" I eked.

"How did you find this place?"

"I don't know!" My words came out frantic. "A voice woke me up and told me to come outside. I just followed it."

"Here. The voice told you to come here?" he yelled.

"It said to come outside, but then I saw a light and I—"

Rook let out a loud growl and reached past me, pushing open the door. "You want to spy on me, then see. I have nothing to hide." He gave me a push, too, and I stumbled inside. The lights came on, blinding me for a moment. Within the space of a few breaths I realized this wasn't a structure to cover a stairwell. It was a single room with cement walls and a twin bed in the corner. A single exposed bulb dangled above an old wooden desk that sat in front of a bookshelf filled with dusty old texts. A small bathroom, with a washbasin instead of a sink and one of those toilets with a raised tank and pull cord, were the only other things in this space.

I turned to Rook, who stood in the doorway, wearing a snug black T-shirt and dark pants. He folded his arms over his broad chest and the ropes of muscles on his forearms strained with angry tension.

"What is this place?" I asked apprehensively.

"What the hell do you think it is?"

"I don't have a damned clue." My eyes darted around the dirt-floored room. "An old monk's dwelling you preserved for posterity?"

"No. My dwelling."

"You—you live here?"

He made a curt nod, his eyes drilling into me.

"But what about your house?"

"I think you're smart enough to know, Stephanie, monks do not get to live in mansions. Nor do they sleep on ten-thousand-dollar mattresses covered in silk sheets."

"Okay, but this? This is—it's awful." Oddly, what saddened me most was the thought of him being here alone with nothing to keep him company but these dusty books. No one should live in such a dreary place.

"*This* reminds me of who I truly am and why I am here," he said.

I nodded hesitantly. "And just why are you here, again?"

"This is the last truly sacred place in this world." His voice came out like a mixture of strength and resentment. "I keep it that way."

"But why you?" I wanted to genuinely comprehend.

"Why not me?"

"Because living like this can't make you happy,"

I said sympathetically.

"Just as life can be beautiful and joyous, it can also be cruel and ugly."

Yeah. I got that. "So you suffer quietly, living in one of the most luxurious places I've ever seen, and you chalk it up to 'misery is just part of life'?" I made little air quotes for emphasis. "That doesn't make any sense."

"I am no more happy or miserable than you or any of the guests who come to this island and have everything the material world can offer."

I guess he had a point, but…"It just bothers me to see anyone live like this." It was a garden shed, at best.

"I live on a beautiful island. That I own. I wake up every morning knowing my purpose, and I have every tool and resource required to see it through. Even by your shallow modern standards, I am a wealthy man. By my standards, I have everything I could ever need."

I got what he was trying to say; however, this looked like some sort of self-imposed punishment. There was no air-conditioning, no fan, no comforts. The floor was made of dirt. The roof appeared to be made of rusted-out tin sheets. And now that I looked closely, the bed was a cement slab with a blanket over it. I knew he lived by some other belief system, one he hadn't fully explained, but did he truly think that living in such dire conditions was his duty? I mean, yes, I wasn't ignorant. There were

examples of people all around the world who chose
the monastic life—Tibetan, Buddhist, Trappist. But
those people had each other, whereas Rook was all
alone because, according to him, there was no one
from his monastery left. So whatever he believed,
whichever religion he suffered for, he did it alone.
No community, no family, no one who truly knew
him.

"I think you're wrong about my definition of
wealth," I said. "To me, it's getting to share your life
with people you love. And, if you're lucky, you find
someone who understands and loves you more than
anyone else. If you're *very* lucky, you get to have a
family or grow old together."

He stared at me for a long moment. And then
another. I could see the hunger in his eyes. I could
feel his desire to touch me. Then it quickly turned
to something I didn't expect: anger.

"Then by your own standards, you've proclaimed yourself impoverished," he threw back in a
stale tone.

I narrowed my eyes. "What's that supposed to
mean?"

"You wear your suffering like a goddamned
badge, an excuse not to live the life given to you. At
least my suffering has a damned purpose. It means
something more than an excuse to whine and hide
out here on my island. So how about you stop
judging me and take a good hard look in the
fucking mirror, Miss Fitzgerald?"

My jaw dropped and my heart felt heavy. It wasn't true, and if it were, he was to blame, because I couldn't move on until I knew the truth—something he had no intention of giving me. Worse yet, he'd stolen the only thing in this world that truly meant anything: my sister. She had been my second mother, my home.

"How about you go fuck yourself, you lonely, fucking bastard," I snarled.

My words visibly enraged him—hard eyes, a snarl on those lips, and a glare to end all glares.

He slammed the door behind him and closed the gap, leaving nothing but hot fury between our warm sweaty bodies. "What you really mean is that you want *me* to fuck you. Isn't. That. Right. Stephanie? You want me to fill that aching void between your thighs because touching me makes you forget how sad and miserable you are."

I backed up until I hit the cool plaster wall. I stared up into those hypnotic sky-blue orbs with silver flecks. I did want him. But now it was like this pull coming from some hateful place deep inside that wanted him to sin and regret it as much as I wanted him to enjoy it. I wanted him to loathe himself as he took me, knowing it was wrong. I wanted him to love it so much that he'd come back for more so then I could deny him.

I smiled up at him. "Yes."

He stilled for the space of three lust-filled heartbeats and then grabbed me by the shoulders.

"You're going to regret this." His mouth was hard and demanding on mine as he pushed past my lips and took the kiss.

I didn't shrink back. When I was done with him, he would despise himself and dream about nothing but being inside me for the rest of his goddamned solitary life.

I clawed at his shirt, half lifting, half tearing it away. He did the same to me, only breaking our spite-filled kiss long enough to remove my pink T-shirt. My fingertips dove for the front of his waistband, wedging between his pants and the coarse hair just above his shaft. I didn't unbutton. I tore and shoved until his rock-solid cock was bare to me and warm against my belly. He had no trouble shimmying down my stretchy loose shorts and panties, leaving me naked.

He pulled back and looked at my body for a split second, a furious hunger in his eyes. For a moment, I thought he might stop. Shockingly, I feared it. I wanted this.

Instead of stopping, he spun me around and grabbed my hands, pushing my palms to the wall. "Don't you fucking say a word."

I braced myself as his hand slid between my legs, his thick fingers parting my folds before he shoved them in. I gasped at the delicious intrusion. Rook. Inside me. Not his dick, but what did that matter? His body was inside mine, thrusting, feeling, enjoying the wetness that came from my lust for him.

"You fucking like that?" he growled. "You like thinking that I need you and want you. But really *you* need me. And when we're done, you always will. They all do," he said ominously.

All. They all *do?* A cold chill swept through my bones. While the penetration of my body felt sinfully delicious, his words did not. They were an intrusion of my soul.

"Wait," I said, trying to turn and get him off me just as I felt him thrust his hard cock inside.

I gasped from the pain, from him going too deep.

"This is what you wanted." He bucked his hips, triggering another sharp pain. "To fill me with hate and self-loathing." He pressed his chest firmly into my back, pinning me to the wall. His cock pulled out and slammed into me again. "But I could never hate myself for fucking you. I would only hate you."

"Stephanie?" A cold slap across my cheek jarred my body like an ice pick to the heart.

I sucked in a sharp breath, my fingers fisting the fabric beneath me, my eyelids exploding open. *Oh, shit. Oh, shit.*

"Where am I?" I felt something rough beneath my back and the heat of the blinding sun on my eyelids, coming through a small window.

Rook leaned over me, frowning. "I think the bigger question is: Why are you here? In your underwear?"

With dread, I slowly looked down, finding my body stretched across the length of a narrow bed. I wore nothing but my white tank top and pink lacy thong. My eyes shuffled around the sparsely decorated room with smooth plaster walls, a rickety old desk and chest, and five plank wood shelves filled with dusty books.

What the hell?

Terrified, I returned my gaze to Rook, not knowing how I'd gotten to this place or managed to dream of it. I'd never been here.

Horror filled me. The feeling of not being in control of my mind and body was as close to hell as I ever wanted to come.

My eyes teared up, and Rook's expression turned from stern to something more sympathetic.

"Another of your dreams, I assume." He shook his head and sighed exasperatedly. "What am I going to do with you, Miss Fitzgerald?" he murmured, staring affectionately into my eyes.

"I don't know." *Because I think I'm going mad.*

He smiled with pity. Or compassion. Or regret. Who knew?

"Neither do I." He drew a shallow breath and released it, infusing a sigh into his quiet words. "But you have a home here as long as you like. At least I can give you that."

My tears turned to a silent sob. How this man knew exactly what my heart ached for, I didn't know. But he did. It was his gift.

He stood from the bed and looked down at the dirt floor. "It's my fault that she's gone. I should've had more security that night, and for this, I am sorry. I wish I could give you more." He headed for the door.

I got up, grabbing the rough gray blanket from the bed to cover myself. "Wait. Where are you going?"

"I cannot be around you when you're…like this." He swallowed the words.

"Like what?" I mumbled, guessing he referred to my mental instability.

"So in need of me." He looked away, his jaw clenching. "There is a robe in the chest in the corner you may borrow. In fact, anything on this island is yours, if you wish. Anything except the one, of course."

The one. Himself.

My body shook with the urge to stop him from leaving—I didn't want to be alone—but I held myself back and watched the door close behind him.

I felt completely scrambled, and it wasn't entirely due to the nightmare. It was that Rook had been right. As much as I hated to admit it, the one thing I needed in this moment was him. The strange connection between us soothed me. He was like an addiction.

But why would I have feelings for such a bad man?

Maybe he's not bad. Maybe I'd convinced myself

that I'd seen strange things simply because I'd wanted an excuse to stay. Rook had said that I wanted to hide from the world, I wanted to suffer. But that had been me speaking, a product of my own dreams.

Goddammit. I felt like every step I took got me further away from the truth and brought me closer to my own demise. Because my heart was broken, and so was I. Yet, for a moment, when Rook offered me a home, I'd felt hope again.

CHAPTER SEVEN

I don't know how long I stood there staring at the dirt floor, my mind attempting to sort through the chaos, but once I picked myself up, I decided to look at a few texts from the shelves. Many were handwritten in Latin on old yellowing paper. *Maybe journals.* There weren't any chapters or headers. Some were printed books written in Greek, Latin, and French. The scrolls were a mixture of the same.

"Guess I know why he didn't kick me out," I mumbled, sitting at Rook's old desk, wrapped in his brown wool robe that smelled like a mixture of his cologne and earth. There was nothing in this room I could read, and if by some chance I spoke French or Latin, I guessed the languages weren't modern versions.

Or maybe he really truly doesn't give a shit. He was beginning to convince me that he didn't have anything to hide, and that I'd made up stories in my mind just to cope. *Or to distract myself.*

I took the last scroll, carefully rolled it up and placed it back on the shelf. I sat on his lumpy hard bed and began contemplating my next move.

Well, I wasn't in a position to throw in the towel. I had to ladder up and think about my options. I could leave and try to put the past behind me, but I would still have to deal with Warner. He'd given me one hundred thousand dollars in exchange to be his inside "man" and help him buy or steal Rook's Island. I knew I could return the money—Rook said he would refund my guest fee—but that wouldn't suffice. Warner wanted the island for money laundering or drug smuggling or whatever that man did for a living. I *could* make up a lie about the island already belonging to someone he didn't want to mess with or tell him it had legal problems—the sort Warner would not want to drag himself into—but those came with risks, too. A man like Warner might kill me anyway simply for having wasted his time.

No, going home empty-handed didn't seem like a great choice, though, it was a choice.

The next option would be to allow myself to believe that Rook was a good guy, and the things I'd seen or that feeling in my gut were nothing but my own fiction. I could live here indefinitely and hope Warner Price never found me. But then he'd go after my friends. Maybe Dad, too. *Not an option.*

The final choice was to keep going and trust the feeling in my gut telling me this was all a sham and that something unnatural was happening here. Something Rook didn't want me to find out. *Maybe Cici found out. Maybe Rook couldn't let her go home.*

I sat for another long moment, every cell in my body playing tug-of-war. Being deceitful wasn't in my nature. Neither was revenge, at the end of the day.

So what did I really want? *I guess justice for Cici.*

I drew a slow breath. Okay, I had less than two weeks to shake the truth from this place. I would push as hard as I could—push Rook's patience to see if I could get him to crack or slip up, push the staff to trust me, push myself to keep it together. I would *not* lose focus. I would *not* think about the sound of Rook's voice just now when he told me he wanted to give me a home. I would *not* think about how the air left my lungs when he entered a room or how pained he'd looked when he knew I needed him.

I stood and tightened the sash of the robe around my body. The thing was so long that a foot of fabric puddled on the ground.

"How can he stand wearing this?" I scratched my neck and arm. *Wool in the jungle.* And how strange he'd let me borrow it. On the other hand, he'd literally said I could have anything on this island. Anything except him.

I opened the rickety wooden door, and a beam of sunlight sliced through the room. I looked down and noticed something solid beneath a thin film of loose dirt. I kicked at it with my bare foot and then bent over, sweeping away the loose soil to find a flat metal hook drilled into the surface of something.

What the hell is this? I pulled, and a square, three-foot-by-three-foot panel lifted, exposing an opening.

I got on all fours and lowered my head inside. There wasn't much light, but I could see a narrow ladder leading down.

Ohmygod. This has to be it.

I quickly turned myself around and descended. It took several long moments for my eyes to adjust, but the moment they did, I knew what this was: Rook's real home.

Fucking liar.

It didn't take long to find the light switch or the room with monitors not dissimilar to the one in the offices. Only this one had a view of the office spaces themselves, the staff common areas in the apartment complex, people's living rooms—including mine and Luke's—the docks, shorelines, and everything inside Rook's mansion.

He was *watching me when I'd stayed there*. I didn't see views of the bathrooms—thankfully—but he'd been able to watch me when I slept and now when I worked.

All right. This merely confirmed what I'd already suspected and he'd partially confessed to once—he kept an eye on things.

Carefully, I closed the door and went to the

next room. It was his bedroom—comfortable and clean with beige tile flooring, a king-sized bed covered in white linens, and a closet filled with expensive suits. A full-length beveled mirror hung on one wall and an abstract painting of a red butterfly on the other. I studied the painting's violent splashes of flaming reds and oranges exploding from a sea of deep blues, almost like a butterfly escaping an icy hell.

A ribbon of goose bumps fluttered down my arms, and I jumped, sweeping my hands over the skin. There was nothing there, but, *Goddammit, this fucking island! Creepy to the core.* I shut off the lights and went to the last room at the end of the hall. My fingertips found the switch, and with a flick, I nearly fell sideways.

Holyfuck. I stepped inside the cavernous room containing rows and rows of books and a spiral staircase in the corner.

"Oh my God." I walked to the wrought-iron railing and leaned over. *One, two, three…* I counted ten floors beneath me. *What is this?*

My bare feet clapped down the stairs, and I skidded off the last step. Shelves extended as far as the eye could see in every direction. The entire floor had to be the size of four tennis courts.

"And there are ten of these?" I muttered to myself.

I grabbed the first book I came to and looked it over. It was thin, like a ledger, with numbers on the spine.

I cracked it open to the first page.

Meg Purdue
Age: Forty-four
Fantasy request: Scottish Castle
Guest description: Meg is recently divorced.
Her daughter just graduated from college.

I slapped the book closed and went for the next, my eyes scanning frantically. *Emily Johannsson*. Her profile mentioned her shyness and the request to have the Tarzan fantasy.

Okay. Wow. These were guest records.

I walked to the spiral staircase and once again leaned over. There had to be hundreds of thousands of books to dig through. I would have to come back later when I knew Rook was tied up for several hours.

I turned to leave, but stopped. The books were in order of the visit dates. I quickly shuffled through the row corresponding to my group from last week.

My record wasn't there, and upon inspection of Cici's group, neither was hers.

CHAPTER EIGHT

"Hey, where you been? Thought we were going to work out," said Luke, making himself a cup of coffee as I came through the door, all buzzing with adrenaline. I'd found something. Something that might soon bring this nightmare of a situation to a close.

His eyes washed up and down my body. "Please don't tell me you went to the gym without me, wearing that."

I glanced down at the enormous, oversized brown robe covering my body. "Errr…no."

I headed straight for my bedroom, closed the door, and spotted my pajama bottoms on the bed. So I'd literally stripped in my sleep and then walked across the entire island in my thong. *What the hell is the matter with me?*

I blew out a breath. I couldn't keep doing this.

I threw on my PJ shorts and headed back into the living room. "Where can I buy a lock for my door?"

Wearing a gray tee and black exercise shorts, Luke stopped stirring his coffee and blinked at me with his big hazel eyes. "Have I done something wrong?"

"Oh, no. I didn't mean for the inside of my room. I meant for the outside. I want you to lock me in every night."

He frowned with a disturbed expression. "I've heard a lot of strange requests from women, but that's a new one."

"I sleepwalk," I explained. "And apparently I'm now doing it in my underwear."

Luke set his spoon on the breakfast counter. "Really? Did you do it last night?" He sounded excited.

I nodded.

"And I missed it?"

I tilted my head to the side and flattened my lips.

His smile dropped. "Sorry. Yes. We can get you a lock. I'm sure the maintenance crew has plenty. But are you sure you want me to lock you in every night? What if you have to use the bathroom or there's a fire?"

"I'll manage." I really couldn't allow this place to take over my mind in the nocturnal hours like it had been. Especially since there was no explanation for why it was happening.

"Okay," he said hesitantly. "But I'll unlock you as soon as I get up for the gym—I don't always come back afterward."

"Thank you." I stared absentmindedly at his

cup of coffee, thinking about Rook's underground room. Why keep all of the records there? And on paper?

"Want some coffee?" Luke asked, noticing the direction of my gaze.

"Oh, no, thank you. I was just thinking about my new role. I'm supposed to screen guests before they come on the island, but don't we have a lot of repeat customers?"

"Sure. Half the people who come are regulars."

Doing some rough math, if the island hosted about twenty guests a week, that came out to around one thousand visitors a year, but half were repeats. That meant Rook added about five hundred new records each year. There had to have been at least five thousand records on just one floor of that library—that equated to ten years' worth. *And there are ten floors in that library.*

"Has Rook ever mentioned how long he's been in business?" I asked, just to see what Luke might say.

Luke shrugged. "Not sure. You should ask him."

"Yeah. Of course. I was really just thinking aloud," I lied.

"Well, lucky you. Listening is my specialty." He took another sip of coffee.

Luke's words triggered another thought. Now that I knew Rook had a camera in here, it finally made sense that we'd been roomed together. Rook believed there was an attraction between Luke and me, so this situation could only fuel those feelings. Rook wanted us to be close so I'd tell Luke what I was really thinking.

What other reason could there be? None. And this morning had been the kick in the ass I needed. I'd been softening toward Rook again, falling victim to the powerful, sinful feelings he provoked. But now, I knew he'd lied. I knew he was watching me, too.

Okay, so I'll let him watch me and Luke bonding. Rook could listen in and see I wasn't up to anything—I respected his vows; I felt connected to this island and committed to my job. He could trust me. And trust would lead to information.

I smiled at Luke. "So what are you up to today?" I asked cheerily.

"We're salvaging the second yacht. Then we'll start cleaning the fleet and preparing gear for next week."

"Well, I need to take a shower. Maybe we can meet up for lunch? I saw there's a nice beach on the east side of the island, and I can make sandwiches—spotted some delicious peanut butter in the fridge."

Luke shrugged. "Sure. I can bring a few snorkels if you're into that."

I continued smiling. "That sounds fun. And considering where we live, I'm sure you won't mind if I skinny-dip. I seem to have lost my swimsuit." I turned and went into my room, letting that thought simmer in Luke's head. I hoped to God Rook heard that. If not, he'd surely see or hear about my lunchtime skinny-dipping from Luke.

Next, I needed to get ready and head to the office. I would be making some changes in my training program. When I was done with the next week's activities, Rook wouldn't have a doubt in his mind that I was here for one reason and one reason only: to work for him.

I threw on a clean Hawaiian-style shirt and khakis and headed for Rook's tropical Ken-and-Barbie mansion. That was what it reminded me of now. Just a fancy shell made for pretending. It wasn't really his home, as I'd suspected all along.

I opened the front door, peeking in. "Hello?" No one replied, so I entered, closed the door, and headed upstairs. As I passed the bedroom where the woman had been staying, I couldn't help snooping to see what had been left behind.

I cracked open the bedroom door. There wasn't much besides the floral curtains and empty bed. I went over to the closet door and found a few wire hangers left on the floor.

"As I said," Rook's voice came from behind me, "she is gone."

I drew a breath, remembering my renewed pledge to play the role of happy, carefree manager who was here to live, here to stay.

I turned and smiled. "Where did she go?"

He shrugged and looked away. "She didn't say."

A lie. He looked away when he lied.

Wanting to choose my next words carefully, I stared for a moment, trying not to notice the masculine shape of his body, accentuated by the casual clothes he wore today—rumpled navy blue Bermudas that hung low on his narrow hips and a light blue T-shirt that matched his eyes. With the way his clothes hugged the contours of his pecs and muscled thighs, it was difficult to think clearly.

"That hurricane must've really scared her off," I said with a small quiver in my voice. "It was pretty crazy, though I have to admit, you built everything on this island like a fortress." I'd seen very little damage besides a few fallen trees and a lot of branches and leaves.

"Best construction money can buy."

"Kind of like Disneyland," I said.

He smiled and two small divots puckered in his stubble-covered cheeks. "Only naughtier. And for adults."

"Works for me."

"Speaking of, how is the arrangement with Luke suiting you?" he asked.

"Wonderful, actually. I think we'll get along great." I purposely looked away as if I had something to hide, something in the realm of a woman's secret, such as Luke and I were "bonding." Really though, I thought of Rook—naked, his body emerging from the lagoon and drops of water glistening off his tall, chiseled body. His long, thick cock hanging between his tanned thighs. My body instantly flushed and a sensual chill swept through me. I'd never in my life seen a more stunning man. I doubted I ever would.

Feeling my face flush, I drew a breath and returned my gaze to Rook just in time to see him licking those sinful lips.

"So you are happy, then?" he asked with a subtle edge.

"Yes. Aside from the strange sleepwalking. By the way, I'm really sorry about this morning. It must've been a shock to find me there. I mean, I'd never even seen the place."

"Nothing shocks me anymore. But I'm sure you just stumbled upon it as you were wandering the jungle. Either way, I am happy you were not injured, though you did look quite shaken."

Ah yes. He'd said I looked like I needed him. "I was fine once I fully woke up. Really. And I've asked Luke to put a lock on the outside of my door so I don't wander into the ocean or something. Not sure I can sleep-swim."

"Let us not find out. Shall we get on with our day?" He turned and headed for my new office.

"Rook? There's something I need to talk to you about. It's important." I followed him into the office and stopped in the doorway.

"Yes?" He stood behind the desk, reaching for something in the drawer.

"I want to do the fantasies."

His head of dark, thick wavy hair whipped up, but he didn't speak. The aggravated look in his pale eyes said it all.

"Not all of them," I added. "Just the most popular ones."

"Why would you want that?" he spat.

"I think if I'm really going to do this job well, I need to know the product. I need to experience what our guests feel, and immerse myself in the island."

"You were a guest just last week."

He's pushing back. Rook didn't want me sleeping with these men, and I couldn't lie, it felt good knowing he was against it. But there was no room for that little corner of my soft heart anymore. I knew Rook was a con man. I'd seen the proof this morning.

"I was too wrapped up in Cici's death to really experience anything," I explained. "I mean, yes, I saw how well run this place is and how beautiful the men are, but I didn't get into the fun."

He knew that was true. I'd been nothing but a pill while the other guests lived it up, dancing, drinking, swimming, and screwing.

"Why? Is there an issue?" I asked. "Because Luke told me the prior managers were required to do a run-through because you really wanted them to know the fantasies from the inside." I paused. "No pun intended."

His dark brows pulled tightly together. He looked like he might just throttle me. "You are out of your mind if you think—"

"I don't expect special treatment because of our," I toggled my finger between us, "relationship."

"We do not have a 'relationship.'" Rook's nostrils flared, and his chest expanded with several angry breaths, reminding me of a bull ready to charge.

Suddenly, he turned, heading for the door. "I must go and help Luke recover that last boat. We can discuss your onboarding further at another time."

"What do you want me to do all day?" I asked.

"Review the file for next week in the schedules folder. Learn about the guests, memorize their fantasies, read the preparation checklists."

Unable to get away from me fast enough, Rook disappeared from the room, leaving behind a scent of exotic spices and florals. *And Rook.* He smelled so delicious, like he'd gone to a male pheromone factory and had been drenched in sexual temptation.

I resisted inhaling deeply and instead called out, "I'm doing dry runs of the fantasies for next week!"

A few moments later, I heard the front door slam shut.

Jesus. I let go of the tension in my chest and dropped my hands to my sides. A small city could be lit up with the energy left in the room. Rook and I were like two giant spinning magnets. Then it dawned on me. Rook would be tied up for the next few hours. I had to go back to his library. I had to see what else might be down there.

"Motherfucker," I whispered, sweating profusely from my sprint through the damp, hot jungle. Rook had locked the goddamned door. Only, there was no keyhole. Just a plain wood-plank door.

"Sure. *Mi casa, su casa*," I panted, giving the door a spiteful shove.

He either knew I'd found the rest of his little home or he feared I might. I would have to find a way to get back in. Perhaps I could follow him and see where he kept a key. Maybe I'd make up some bullshit story about wanting to hang out here again.

For fuck's sake. Like he'd believe that. It was a hot, musty shack. Only mosquitos wanted to hang out there. I would definitely have to follow him back here tonight. If there was no lock, then he had to open the door somehow.

By the time I returned to my office on the second floor of Rook's mansion by the sea, it was almost ten o'clock in the morning and I had a lot of cramming to do. Grateful for the air-conditioned room, I logged in to the computer and found the schedule for next week along with the guest list.

A full house. Fifteen women would be flying in on Monday, but there would be no VIPs. I wondered if Rook handled them exclusively.

I quickly took notes, listing which fantasies the women would be enjoying. *The harem, the submarine, snowed in with a sexy stranger.* There were also two cowboy fantasies, but one wanted Old West and the other modern-day Wyoming. There were a few requests for the Scottish laird fantasy with a "Jamie look-alike" and a *Game of Thrones* Khal Drogo request.

I cleared my throat. *I wonder if she wants rapy honeymoon Khal or the nicer version?*

The rest were interesting but not surprising— kidnapped sex slave and a Roman gladiator seduction, plus a Captain Hook request.

I looked up from my notepad, staring at the wall. I'd already told Rook I was going to do some of these, but I wasn't sure I really could. In all honesty, I'd only had a few boyfriends, and I'd never enjoyed sex. Something had always been missing with them. Mainly, orgasms. Then, after Cici died, it got worse. I couldn't stand being touched. For months, I experienced panic attacks when anyone so much as brushed against me in passing. Forget about being hugged or shaking hands. The psychologist I visited once and only once told me it had been related to the trauma of losing my sister, that intimacy frightened me.

It wasn't until Rook touched me on my first

night here that I felt something other than painful pinpricks and a rush of fear. His warm hand on the small of my back as we'd danced felt good. It felt right. Then, when he'd kissed me a few days later, for the first time ever I felt the sort of hard aches and throbs I'd only heard about from my girlfriends. Rook had made me want him so badly that I'd nearly come the moment I felt his naked shaft brush against my sensitive bud.

"Gah." I stood from the desk, feeling hot and flustered. My nipples ached and my core fluttered uncontrollably.

But I would not be sleeping with Rook. Not now. Not ever. I *would* be sleeping with strangers, though I knew it would be difficult to enjoy it.

Get it together, Steph. I was a grown woman who had to act like it. This wasn't a game or a movie. This was real. Cici's death was real. Warner was real. If I had to step outside my comfort zone to get what I needed, then so be it.

I took my list and started searching the files on the computer for the fantasy specifications. I read them carefully and then set up time with the area managers to go over the staffing and props checklists. Tomorrow, Wednesday, I'd call a meeting to ensure everything was on schedule and I would schedule my dry runs.

I glanced down at the list of fantasies again. I would go with the least uncomfortable fantasies and pick two—just enough to make Rook believe I was really into this.

Scottish laird and cowboy. Those were popular and they seemed simple enough. I could probably ask the hosts to give me a short version of their dates. In and out. Literally.

My heart began to race at the thought of a strange man's hands on my body, of him inside me.

I am so not cut out for this place. I looked at my watch. It was almost noon and time to meet Luke. One more man I might need to sleep with to make Rook believe I was here for the right reasons so he'd tell me his secrets before my time was up.

Ten minutes later, I arrived in one of the carts to the small beach on the east shore. The white sand and calm turquoise water was the stuff even postcards dreamed of. The thick curtain of lush greenery hadn't been touched by the hurricane, giving the tiny beach a secluded, uninhabited-island feel, like I could very well be the last woman on earth.

I stared out at the ocean, enjoying the warm breeze kissing my cheeks and flowing through the gaps between the buttons of my cotton blouse. It was so peaceful here, so breathtaking that for a moment, I understood why Rook might do almost anything to prevent his home from becoming a Sandals or just another touristy stop for a Carnival Cruise, filled with T-shirt shops and bars. But little did he know that either way, the outcome to all this would involve him losing his island to Warner. Warner would likely turn it into some private gangster oasis with drugs, gambling, and prostitutes. He'd launder his money. He'd kill anyone who got in his way.

Part of me felt guilty about it. The other part of me felt that this was Rook's karma.

I began stripping off my clothes, knowing that Luke would be here at any moment, and I couldn't afford to lose my nerve. Rook wanted me to have a fling with Luke, then that was what I'd do. I'd show I trusted him. I'd tell him things, knowing Rook listened in.

I pulled off my blouse and shorts and then did away with my bra and panties. The wind picked up just enough to make the calm waters chop a bit. Carefully, I tiptoed into the bath-like ocean until waist deep.

"Miss Fitzgerald," Rook's deep voice called out.

Oh God. Why is he—I turned my head right as I took a step and something sharp jammed into the arch of my foot. I fell into the water, and a small wave smacked the back of my head. *Sonofabitch! What was that?*

I popped my head from the waves and clutched my burning foot. Rook, still in his same T-shirt and black shorts, charged in after me.

"What in God's name are you doing, woman?" He scooped me up in his powerful arms.

"I was," I grunted out my words, "going to snorkel with Luke."

"Naked?" he barked, wading back to shore, looking ahead and not at my nude body.

"That was the idea."

"Why?"

I had to lie. "It's time for me to embrace the way things are done here. Otherwise, I'll never be of any use to you."

He grumbled something in a language—maybe French—that I didn't understand. "I'm going to set you down. Just stand on one foot so I can get a look at the other."

I went onto my good foot, and Rook kneeled in front of me. I couldn't help blushing. His face was less than a foot from my groin and his eyes kept flittering to that exact spot.

"Lift the foot higher," he barked.

I placed one hand on his broad shoulder to keep from falling, my breasts, ass and everything blowing in the wind.

"What happened to Luke?" I asked.

"He's still tied up with the yacht. He asked if I could stop by and let you know he couldn't come."

Luke knew I'd be here, likely unclothed. *He set me up.*

Still on his knees, Rook straightened his back, desperately trying to avoid looking at the V between my legs.

"Hold still," he grumbled. "I need to remove

my shirt so I can tie it around your foot; there is a deep cut."

He ripped off his shirt, and my breath caught. The deep grooves of his tan chiseled abs, the dark dusting of hair that ran from his navel underneath his waistband, the strong smooth swell of his arms, and of course, his third rails—those muscles that cut diagonally across his lower torso—he was perfect and oh so astoundingly beautiful.

Rook tied the shirt around my foot to keep the pressure on. "That should hold."

He looked up at me, and his gaze instantly shifted, likely in response to whatever he saw in my eyes. Hard lust. Hunger. Appreciation.

His pale blue-gray eyes slowly drifted down my neck to my breasts. I could almost feel his hands touching my skin, leaving a trail of goose bumps in their wake. His eyes went lower and my breathing became faster. He studied my stomach and hips, and then lower. He stared at the valley between my legs, his chest rising and falling quickly with his own breath.

"You're going to cost me ten lashes tonight, Stephanie," he said, his voice low and gruff.

My nipples hardened. The space between my legs ached and heated. "What would twenty buy you?"

Why had I said that? Why did it take so little for me to forget everything I was here for?

His cool stare snapped to my eyes, a look of

turmoil in them. "Not nearly enough."

Slowly, he rose to his feet and grabbed my pile of clothes from a few feet away. "Here." He handed them over, averting his gaze. "Put these on, and I'll get you to our doctor."

Without a word I dressed. My hands were shaking. I felt light-headed with lust. This was not good.

"Ready," I said with an unsteady voice.

Once again, Rook avoided eye contact, but swooped me into his arms.

I needed to say something. Something that would make him believe I was here to work and meant it.

"I'm sorry you had to see me like this." I stared at his face—that strong jaw inked with black stubble, the elegant curve of high cheekbone.

"I am not. I quite enjoyed it."

What? "Why do you keep toying with me like that, Rook? Is this some game to you?"

He stopped in the soft white sand, clutching me in his arms as if I weighed nothing. "My apologies. You are right. I drew the line. I should maintain it."

"Drawing a line. Is that what you call it?"

He looked at me with furrowed dark brows.

"You're the master of the mind fuck, Rook. You say make yourself at home, you say you want to help, but…" I pulled myself back. I was losing control again.

"But what?"

I smiled to cover my deep-seated frustration.

"Never mind."

"Tell me."

"What's the point?" *I'm only going to lie to you.*

"The point is I asked."

I drew a breath, knowing I had to say something. "I now recognize what happened between us last week wasn't real. Because you're just a fantasy like anything else on this island. You play a part, you let people see what they need to see, you say what they want to hear. But that's not really you, and I get that now. So how could anything I felt for you have been real?" *Basically, I'm over you.*

He stared into my eyes for a long moment, and then, without warning, he kissed me.

Whoa. I wasn't dreaming. Not this time. I hadn't gotten into bed or hit my head. Rook's soft warm lips were on mine, his hot tongue playing against the seam of my mouth. *Why is he kissing me?* I didn't know, but I couldn't stop from melting into it. His tongue slid between my lips, allowing me to taste him.

Sweet. Delicious. My body instantly ached for more.

I wrapped my arms around his neck, deepening the kiss, our tongues sinfully dancing.

How does a monk learn to kiss like a sinner? Because Rook definitely moved like a bad boy. I couldn't get enough.

With our mouths pressed tightly together, the pace of our kissing accelerated. I moved my hands to the sides of his rough cheeks, savoring the feel of having him close while he devoured me, breathing into me.

Suddenly, he set me down and wrapped his arms around my waist, pulling me tightly against his tall, muscular frame, allowing me to feel the steely heat of his erection seeping through our clothes.

Our panting turned into muted groans as our hands began exploring, clawing and grabbing. He leaned over me, cupping my ass and lifting.

Yes, that was what I wanted.

I wrapped my legs around his waist, completely absorbed in him and this moment, of us exchanging the heat of our bodies. Though I bounced in his arms as he walked, the feverish kissing continued, consuming all rational thought.

When the rough bark of a palm tree hit my back, I grunted with pleasure. Not from the bark digging between my shoulder blades but because I felt the force of his hard cock pressing through my shorts.

Fully clothed, he moved his hips, grinding against my c-spot. I moaned with pleasure, and he grunted with his. Soon, he broke the kiss as our hips and bodies found a sinful rhythm leading only to one place.

"Look at me," he commanded in a low voice, his hips bucking hard between my legs.

I opened my eyes, feeling lost in the depths of his gaze while our bodies moved together. I didn't have words for what I felt, but I knew what I wanted with all my heart: for there to be a reason for the emotions stirring inside me.

"Fucking hell, you'll be the death of me, Stephanie," he said, staring into my eyes.

He pushed one last time, and I exploded, coming with every nerve, muscle, and cell of my body, everything freezing in time, everything fading and illuminating all at once. The sinful contractions spiked through me like a bolt of electricity, and I pushed back my head, crying out his name.

Rook's deep voice growled out an animalistic sound as he pressed his entire body into me.

I opened my eyes, wanting to watch him come, to see what his beautiful face looked like when he was lost in the moment. It was sexy beyond words. Uninhibited, masculine, and vulnerable all rolled into one. With his guard down, Rook was even more gorgeous.

My eyes teared up, but I quickly swept the moisture away. I couldn't let him see me like this. Wanting him so much.

With his eyes closed, Rook bent his forehead to mine, his chest heaving. He released my legs and then planted a lazy kiss on my now swollen lips, his strong hands cupping the nape of my neck.

"Why do you make me question every choice I've ever made and every choice forthcoming?"

Forthcoming. A word no one used anymore. A word from another time.

"Who *are* you?" I asked.

He opened his pale eyes and gazed tenderly into mine. "Today I am a sinner." He smiled softly. "Come. I need to get you to our doctor. And I'm in need of a shower and fresh clothes." He held out his hand.

Clearly he wanted to lighten the mood. But I could see the darkness lurking behind his eyes.

"How many lashes?" I asked.

"Enough. But that is not your concern."

CHAPTER NINE

In silence, Rook brought me to the main reception building, on the north side of the island near the landing strip, where the resident physician had an office and exam room around back.

Rook got out of the cart and walked around. We hadn't exchanged a single word since the beach, so to say the situation felt awkward was a huge, huge understatement. We'd just gone at it with our clothes on in some twisted attempt to blow off steam.

But I don't feel relieved. I felt hungrier than ever. He'd given me a taste of something I'd been begrudgingly aching for, and now I wouldn't be satisfied until I had the real thing.

He extended his hand to help me out of the golf cart, but I didn't take it.

"Why don't you just quit?" I asked.

He dropped his hand and rubbed the back of his neck, giving it some thought. "That's like asking you to stop your lying, sneaky games, and to let go of your Cici conspiracy theories."

I bit down on my lower lip. My heart pounded

with adrenaline. I wasn't shocked by his suspicion, but I was shocked that he'd confront me like this. What did he think I'd do, confess?

"I don't know what you mean," I said.

He flashed a smile, making those two deep dimples appear in his stubbled cheeks. "Sure you don't," he said sarcastically. "Just like you don't know more than you should about me."

Rook is tipping his hand. This felt like a test to see if he could trust me. I had to tip my hand, too, and let him in, or he wouldn't do the same.

"I like to know who I'm getting into bed with," I said. "Can you blame me?"

Rook shook his head, as if to say again, *"You're going to be the death of me, woman."*

"I meant it metaphorically—of course," I added. "You want me to stay long term and help you run things, right?"

He stared for the longest moment, his eyes intense and charged with dark emotion. "That is the plan, Miss Fitzgerald." He held out his hand, and this time I took it.

As our palms met, electricity pulsed through me. It was him. *Just because I'm sexually attracted to him doesn't change anything. Don't forget it, Stephanie.* I wouldn't. This episode might have felt good, but really I had to see it for what it was: an opportunity. I'd found another way to get him to trust me.

"Thank you," I said.

"For what?" he asked.

"For giving me my first orgasm. Now that I've had a taste, I'm sure I'll need another." No, I wasn't a virgin, but I'd never experienced that before. Not even on my own.

He gave me a harsh look. "I don't know if my back can handle it." Meaning, he'd be whipping the hell out of himself for what he'd just done.

I flashed a wicked little smile. "I've got a date with a Scottish laird if you're not up for it." Rook needed to be pushed. I couldn't let him put distance between us again, and if I'd learned anything, it was that Rook might feel conflicted about it, but he did want me.

Rook shook his head, and I wrapped my arm around his shoulder. "You're playing with fucking fire, Stephanie."

"Good. I like the heat. Yours especially."

Dr. Rosy was a portly woman in her late sixties, with dark olive skin and bottle-cap glasses. With just one look, I knew she had been living here a long time. Nobody vibed that laid-back and lived near civilization.

"My, my, what have we here?" said Dr. Rosy, emerging from what appeared to be a supply closet.

"She cut her foot—a piece of coral, I think," said Rook.

The doctor bobbed her head. "Did you rinse it with anything?" she asked him.

Rook had a slight blush to his cheeks. "I was too busy taking care of her other needs." He cracked a hint of a smile at me, but then returned to his usual stone-cold façade that gave nothing away. "And now I must take care of my own." He dipped his head and turned toward me. "I leave you in good hands."

"Will I see you later?" I asked.

"I'm afraid I will be quite occupied this evening." His expression remained cool, but I got the gist: penance time.

"I still have your robe. Do you need it?" I smirked with a twinge of sadistic joy. Yes, maybe I was liking the sudden shift in our cat and mouse relationship.

He tilted his head to one side. "Keep it. A souvenir."

"That's really not the sort of thing that does it for me." I flashed a glance down to his bare ripped abs.

"In that case, you may bring it by another time."

"Don't forget my supplies, Rook," said Dr. Rosy. "I can't start the week without smelling salts, saline drips, and sterile ice packs."

"I won't forget," he said all too charmingly.

"Where are you going?" I asked.

"Stateside—I must attend to some personal business. I leave first thing in the morning."

So Rook was leaving me here all alone. I would definitely need to spy on him tonight so I'd know how to access his shack and the library below.

"You will hold down the fort, Miss Fitzgerald, will you not?" he asked.

I nodded. "I'll be working hard on preparing myself for Monday's guests and *personally* inspecting the castle and cattle ranch." I wanted him to think I would still be sampling the Scotsman and cowboy.

He frowned with those cool eyes. "I never said yes to that."

"I never asked for permission."

"I must go." He snarled. "You and I will revisit this topic another time."

I turned my attention to Dr. Rosy. "So how many stitches?"

Rook slipped out, leaving behind his unhappy energy.

Dr. Rosy smiled at me. "What on God's green earth did you do to that man?"

I shrugged, thinking about how he and I had just dry humped each other. I imagined he enjoyed it as much as I did, but that walking around afterwards wasn't his idea of something dignified grown men did. *Or monks.*

Suddenly, I wondered if that was the first time a woman had made him come. *Is he a virgin?*

No. Not possible. Then again, if he truly was what he said, he actually might be.

The thought made me instantly hot. Having

Rook all to myself. Untouched. Pent up. Fucking hotter than hell.

"I don't know," I muttered, unintentionally answering Rosy's question.

She shook her head. "Well, I've never seen Mr. Rook so giddy."

Giddy? One corner of his mouth had curled up.

"I barely know him, so I couldn't say," I replied.

"I've known him for forty years. He was definitely giddy."

Forty. But Rook didn't look older than…than…well, it was hard to say. Sometimes he looked like he was in his early thirties, sometimes in his mid-forties.

"Oh, did you deliver him?" I asked.

"Heavens no. We've only—" She stopped herself midsentence. Dr. Rosy suddenly didn't look so rosy any more. "You know, maybe I misspoke. I've only known him for twenty. The mind hits sixty and it's all downhill from there." She motioned for me to come into her exam room. "Let's get that foot looked at."

Confused, my ass. She was lying. Just like Rook. Just like everyone else on this fucking pile of pretty dirt. She had known Rook for forty years, which meant he was much older than he looked.

I smiled, not wanting to alarm her. "Thanks. It really hurts."

"We'll have you good as new in no time at all."

I hopped up on the exam table. "I hear that's

the specialty on the island."

She smiled with a bit of disdain seeping from her watchful brown eyes. "Why, yes. Nothing like a bit of relaxation in paradise to make you feel years younger."

I cocked my head. "Or a few decades."

She gave me a nod with a snarling grin. "Now that's a little too much to hope for, but one can always wish. After all, this *is* the island of fantasies." She turned away.

ॐ ॐ

Rosy put three stitches in the arch of my foot and then told me to stay off it for a week to ten days. I knew that wasn't going to happen, because tonight I needed to keep watch at Rook's, so I asked her to tape it up good.

I hobbled out of Dr. Rosy's office, surprised to find Luke waiting for me in a golf cart on the path.

"Hey, I heard you need a ride," he said, flashing one of his trademark smiles.

"Don't even," I snapped, walking toward him.

"Even what?"

"You stood me up for our lunch date."

"I did no such thing. Didn't Rook tell you?" he said.

"Tell me…?"

"He made me stay—said I had to inspect the yacht and make a list of repairs."

I slipped into the golf cart, letting that one sink in. "But aren't you a scuba diver?"

"Yes. And we have a harbormaster and maintenance crew who know those boats inside and out."

So Rook made Luke stay behind for nothing, which meant he *had* been listening in on the conversation at our apartment—the one where I told Luke I didn't have a swimsuit.

"I think you should take another apartment, Stephanie," Luke said, driving on the path that cut between two old cedar trees and led to a narrow bridge. I'd learned that this resort was really more like two islands divided by a very narrow channel. During low tide, the channel became rocky tide pools.

"What? Why?" Luke was my pawn now, and I needed him on my chessboard.

"Whatever's going on between you and the boss, I don't want to get caught in the middle. I happen to like my job very much. And as beautiful as you are, there are plenty of other fish who swim to the island." He looked at me. "No offense."

"None taken. But there's no game between me and Rook," I lied, unsure of what else to say.

"Then what would you call it?" he asked.

It's a war, I suppose.

"Nothing. We're nothing to each other."

"And I'm a bald eagle," he muttered.

I didn't respond. Whatever he thought about us didn't matter. And now that Rook and I had become a little more intimate, maybe I didn't need him.

Luke took me back to the mansion so I could return to work and prepare for next week's arrivals. I would have to ask the boss about his screening process and the check-in procedures. I would also inquire about his VIPs, too. Who were they? Where was that manifest?

Okay. I wasn't stupid. I knew he wasn't going to tell me, but I wondered what bullcrap he might spin. I was beginning to see that Rook's lies always told a story:

"Sure. Stay in my cabin, I have nothing to hide." *Really, I don't want you there and have everything to hide.*

"Room with Luke. I don't want you." *Don't you dare think of touching him. I want you.*

"I am the one thing on this island you cannot have." I thought that one over for a moment, my mind drifting back to how Rook had made me insane with lust. Even now. Not bad for a man who likely had never been with a woman. Which might explain why he had the energy of an eighteen-year-old. Of course, he was older, but by how much? Fifty? Sixty? I thought of the eighty-year-old women who had showed up on evacuation day, looking twenty.

My heart thumped against my ribs. *Could Rook be that old? Eighty. Or a hundred—like his library records?*

No. Not possible. But I knew what I'd seen.

That evening, I returned to the apartments and then, deciding I'd had enough of Luke's peanut butter and protein bars, I hobbled to the cafeteria for dinner. It was a large bright room, with a few flat screens set to the news and several colorful sitting areas with coffee tables and comfy couches. Five large tables sat in the center of the room to accommodate groups. Everything was spotless. Everything looked delicious, including the salad bar.

The way of the Rook, as Luke had said.

There was also a grill that served hot meals—all healthy stuff—and several refrigerators filled with prepared or microwavable foods.

I loaded up my tray with a whole-wheat turkey sandwich and an apple, not wanting to carry much given my fresh injury.

"Hey, you're Miss Fitz, right?" said a guy about my age with curly brown hair and the biggest muscles I'd ever seen. Maybe too big.

"Call me Stephanie. When Rook's not around," I added.

"I'm Samuel. Nice to meet you." He went on to explain that he rotated through fifty different fantasies, but specialized in anything violent or bloody.

"Requires a special skill set to make it look real,"

he said. "I'm especially great with explosions. Big. Explosions." He winked.

Oh. That kind of explosion. TMI.

"Okaaay. I will try to remember that," I said, attempting to be open-minded. "See you around."

Not in the mood for being social, I hobbled back toward the elevators. "Hey! It's Fitz!" this guy popped off right as I passed a table of eight men. All huge. All handsome, of course, and all rowdy.

"So I'm guessing that's my new nickname, huh?" *Miss Fitz. Sounds like a cat.* "But please call me Stephanie."

The men introduced themselves, but they all went so fast, I only caught a few names.

"We do the water-related fantasies—sailboats, submarine, Navy recon missions, and jet skis," said the one with brown hair seated closest to me.

"Oh, you guys are the pirates," I said.

"Arrrr!" they all replied in unison.

"Well, nice to meet you," I said. "I'm sure we'll be seeing a lot of each other."

They all laughed.

"That's a polite way of saying it," said a tall blond a few seats down. "I'm Brad, by the way." He stood and proceeded to unzip the front of his shorts. "Sure you don't want to take a look now."

"Ohmygod." I held out my hand, not at all amused.

"Didn't they tell you?" he said.

"Tell me what?"

"You'll do the grooming inspection." He wiggled his golden brows.

Dear God. "Yes. Actually, Mr. Rook mentioned something about inspections." I leaned in. "But will I really have to look at your…penises?"

They all laughed hysterically, bowing over their plates of food.

Brad gave me a consoling look. "Don't worry, you'll get used to it. You'll see so many cocks that it'll be like looking at trees in a forest."

"Big trees! With hairy balls!" one of the guys called out.

"All right then. I'm a dick inspector," I muttered to myself.

"At least you won't get in the way of a good boner," said a huge burly man down at the end of the table, eating an enormous pile of spaghetti.

I frowned.

Brad leaned in to the table. "It didn't help the performances, knowing that Day was watching."

"Oh, fuck that, man," said a guy with cropped blond hair sitting beside him. "One word from her in my earpiece was enough to give me a weeklong softy."

"Nice to know." I drew a breath. "Well, I look forward to—"

"Is it true?" asked Brad. "You're not going to test out the fantasies? Rook said you're taken or something."

Rook said that? It didn't take much for me to

hope that Rook meant something by it and for me to kick myself in the ass for wishing it.

"Uh. No. I'm not taken," I said. "I think there's just some misunderstanding."

The men's faces turned into bonfires of joy.

"Please tell me you're into pirates," said burly guy, "because we're the best."

"I'm afraid I'm not ready for group sex, but I'm sure you're all very…" I tried to think of a word to flatter them, "very good with your swords."

They nodded in agreement.

"Well, if you change your mind, we're here all year round," he said.

Year round. That made me start thinking. "Oh, I'm reviewing our safety protocols. Were you guys here a few months ago when that woman drowned?"

Brad and the rest of the guys gave me blank expressions.

"What? You didn't hear about it?" I asked.

"No. And we have weekly reviews and staff meetings. Anything goes wrong, we all hear about it. Rook takes guest and staff safety very seriously. He fires someone at least once a month for not following protocols."

What the hell? "So no deaths, no drownings?"

"Not that any of us have heard about," said Brad. The men all agreed.

"But if a guest went missing or did drown?" I asked.

"Heads would fucking roll," said Brad. "Rook

wouldn't let that slide."

"Hey," said another guy who had stayed quiet, eating his salad all the way down at the end next to burly guy. "Do you remember three years ago, when that boat capsized? Five women went over and one was never found."

A few guys nodded, agreeing with his recollection.

"What happened?" I asked.

"A sudden storm kicked up and they got caught in it. Rook shut the entire resort down so everyone could help look for the missing woman. He refunded all of the guests' money and sent them home."

"And?" If I were sitting, I'd be on the edge of my seat.

"We never found her. Rook was pissed."

"Not pissed," said Brad. "Rook was devastated. He closed the island for six months."

"But he kept paying us, so whatever," said burly guy.

I didn't know what to say, but who the fuck cared? This was the proof my brain needed, but my heart did not. If Cici had really died like Rook said, then everyone would remember. He would've stopped the world to find her. He claimed he had, but it was just one more lie.

An unforgiveable lie. I nodded solemnly, my heart jumping to the light. Cici might still be alive. No, I quickly jerked myself back. I knew she'd never abandon me, which meant she was dead. *But not how Rook said*—search parties, helicopters, hundreds of people looking.

"Hey, you okay?" asked Brad.

Not even close. "Sure. I'm fine. I guess I got confused about the timing. It's so hard to keep fiction and reality apart when you're here." I gave them a little wave. "See you all soon."

"Hey, Stephanie!" Burly guy at the end stood and grabbed his package. "I'll keep the garden nice and trim for you!" He chuckled.

Real nice. But what should I expect? A perfect gentleman? Gentlemen didn't get up in the morning and rehearse their lines for a voluntary rape and pillage scene. *Fuck this place.*

I turned and held up my pinky, forcing myself to stay in character. "Yes, please keep the hedges neat. Otherwise, I won't be able to spot your blade of grass."

The men all laughed and threw pieces of bread at him.

"Hey! Hey! I'm bigger than you gherkins!" he chided as I exited the cafeteria and proceeded to vomit in a trash can next to the elevators. My eyes filled with big sloppy tears, though I didn't really know why. I'd suspected all along that Rook had been lying, though a part of me had been holding out hope he'd been honest about Cici. I should be relieved that I'd gotten a piece of the truth, not coming undone with grief, feeling like Cici'd died all over again.

Fuck that. I'm done being sad. I had to let go of all that now and release myself from any guilt I might feel over destroying this man. This beautiful, severely fucked-up, evil man who knew exactly what I wanted and needed to hear.

I wiped my mouth with the back of my hand and got into the elevator to go up to my floor. My soul sank deep, my heart sank deeper. I'd never felt so alone in my entire life. My mother, gone. My father fighting a war that existed in his head. My sister taken from me. Now, I realized, hope had been added to my list of the dead.

CHAPTER TEN

"I'm going out," I said to Luke the moment he arrived looking sunburnt and exhausted.

I slid past him. "Be back soon."

"You have stitches in your foot," he yelled as I strode down the hallway, swallowing the pain that lingered inside and out. I'd had over an hour to stew. Now, I was pissed and on the warpath. *Rook never looked for her. Rook never looked for her. He is such a liar. I'm going to kill him. I'm an idiot for hoping. I'm going to kill—*

"Stephanie?" Luke called out. "Are you okay? Where are you going?"

"To the library."

"Library?"

"Absolutely." I jerked open the stairwell door and went up, not hearing whatever it was he yelled. Didn't care. If I was right, Rook had already heard what I'd just said. *Or he'll be getting a call from his boy, Luke.*

Fifteen minutes later, I stood behind a large tree trunk only a few yards from Rook's cabin. Like clockwork, Rook showed. The best part was that he believed I'd already figured out how to get inside, because he didn't hesitate to push the door three times. It sprang open, and he rushed in to look for me.

That's it. Three pushes. It was some sort of programmed pressure lock.

I wanted to stay there and smack the hell out of him when he came out, but the key now was keeping my cool. I'd made a lot of progress these past few days. I had to give myself that.

Carefully, I walked through the dense trees and grabbed the cart I'd left on the path. I headed back to my apartment, where I found Luke pacing nervously in the living room when I entered.

"What are you doing here?" Luke asked the moment he saw me.

Wow, your behavior is not at all suspicious, I thought sarcastically.

"What do you mean?" I replied innocently.

"You said you were going to the library."

I plunked down on the couch. "Yeah, well, apparently there isn't one. I thought the room next to the gym had books."

"You mean the timekeeping room?"

"Oh. Is that what it is? Go figure." I drew a long breath. "Well, my foot hurts, and now I have nothing to read. Guess I'll watch TV in my room. Night!"

Luke eyed me suspiciously. "Wait. We forgot to put a lock on your door. I can call maintenance now and ask what they have."

I thought about it for a moment—I really couldn't be allowed to get up and wander in my sleep. But now he seemed a little too eager to lock me up. *Nuh-uh.*

I turned and headed into Luke's bedroom.

"What are you doing?" he asked.

"I'm sleeping in your bed tonight. Put a chair or something bulky against the door when you come in, would you? That way you'll hear me if I try to get out."

He stared with a bit of panic in his eyes. I guessed what he was thinking. He'd asked me to move out so that he wouldn't get in the middle of me and Rook.

You're already in the middle. He worked for Rook. He helped Rook keep me in the dark.

"Don't worry," I said. "There's nothing going on with our boss. Nothing at all. I'm a free woman, I promise."

Luke bobbed his head slowly, apparently unconvinced.

"Look, I'll ask to be moved to another apartment tomorrow if that's what you really want. But tonight, I need a place to sleep—somewhere safe."

"If I say yes, it's asking for trouble," he said.

"Then don't say yes. Just come to bed." I turned, went into his room, and removed my shorts, not bothering to turn on the lights. "I sleep in just my tank top. Hope you don't mind." If Rook was watching, let him. Let him imagine what I looked like lying in my panties in another man's bed.

I heard a sour grumble from the other room.

Don't care. I settled into Luke's queen-sized bed. The sheets were soft and cool, just like mine. His room, though, had a big bookshelf and a reading chair in the corner. A blue rug on the floor gave the space a much homier feel, as did the old black-and-white photos on the wall.

I turned over on my side and stared at the clock on his nightstand. Rook would be gone in the morning, and I would head straight to his lair. If lucky, I'd find everything I needed and be gone in a week.

At five a.m. sharp the sound of Luke's snoring pulled me from my sleep. I hopped from bed, where he'd erected a wall of pillows between us.

Interesting. On the outside, Luke seemed like this adventurous, ex-military guy who dedicated himself to scuba diving and casual sex. But now I was beginning to see that he cared more about his boss than anything else. At the very least, he didn't want to displease him.

I suddenly wondered what would happen to Luke if Rook lost the island. Would he be forced to leave? Where would he go?

Stop it. I'm sure there are hundreds of resorts that

will take him. Besides, he'd decided on his own to get in bed with Rook. His problem.

I removed the chair Luke had placed in front of the door, careful not to wake him. I stepped out into the living room and tiptoed over to my room to dress. If anyone saw me traipsing through the jungle, I'd say I wanted to go for a walk.

I pulled on a pair of running shorts, sat on my bed, slid on my shoes, and—

Oh shit. My foot. There were no stitches. No bandage. *I'm asleep.* My pulse rate shot up. Unlike the other times, now I was aware that my mind and body were in different time zones, so to speak.

The creak of the front door's hinges caught my attention, almost calling for me. I froze for a moment, my breath coming fast. Every time I dreamed like this, it had led me somewhere important. Somewhere closer to the truth.

I stood slowly, went out into the living room, and through the open front door. If not knowing you were asleep was a trip, knowing was ten times trippier.

Using the stairwell, I went outside where the sun peeked over the tree line. I pivoted in a circle, waiting for a sign. Where was I supposed to go this time? There was no lantern or monk. Or Cici calling out to me.

I decided Rook's cabin was still my best bet. If something important was in there, I would find it.

It didn't take long for me to get inside and take

the ladder to the hidden corridors that led to the library. I took the spiral staircase down and walked the first few floors, noting the numbers on the spines of each book. Before, I'd been too excited to notice that Rook didn't use some Dewey decimal system. The numbers were all dates plus one. *11.15.67.126890.* November fifteenth, 1967. Guest number 126890—according to the page inside one book I grabbed from the shelf.

I rushed to the bottom floor, eager to see the spines of the oldest records, but when I got there, I found the books had changed. They were thicker, their leather spines cracked with age. One in particular had a symbol of a butterfly painted in red.

That one.

I plucked it off the shelf and quickly thumbed through the pages. The language appeared to be Latin, which I couldn't read, but the hand-drawn pictures told bits and pieces of a tragic, violent story. Monks hung from tree branches while black natives looked on, weeping and holding each other. The next chapter, white men on horses waved swords and struck down the men in robes. In the background, a group of women with feathers in their hair looked on in horror. Chapter after chapter told horrible accounts of the monks being slaughtered, the gist being that these men hadn't been welcome anywhere. They'd been hunted like animals.

The final chapter showed the monks in several small boats, rowing to an island. Then there were pages upon pages of text. If this book truly existed, I would have to take photos and translate it. The final pages, however, needed no interpretation.

The ink was a crisp black. *Fresh.* And the drawing showed men slitting the monks' throats or tossing them into a small lake. To the side, a little boy watched the men beating a black woman.

I snapped the book shut and swallowed down the bile. *Rook.* Rook told me he'd lost all but his aunt here on this island. He told me she'd raised him and that the men who did this terrible thing died when their ship sank a mile away. *This little boy is Rook. It has to be.*

I opened the text to the very last page, where there was a drawing of a ship sinking into the ocean while storm clouds raged above. Was this my mind repeating a story Rook had already told me? Or was this really what happened?

It suddenly dawned on me. *That woman.* The black woman who had been living in his house and caught us together that night. Rook had sworn she wasn't a girlfriend or anything like that. Yet she had been livid.

Livid like a mother who didn't approve. She's his aunt.

My heart cramped. That woman had looked young, even younger than Rook.

Fuck. I started to panic. *I have to wake up. I have to come here and see everything with my own eyes! Wake up. Wake up. Wake the fuck up!* I yelled at the top of my lungs.

My eyes flew open, and I hurled upright. "Jesus," I gasped, my mind quickly orienting. *Still in Luke's bed. Thank God.* But there was no Luke, and his side of the bed hadn't been slept in from what I could tell.

I got up, instantly feeling a sharp pain in my foot. *Thank God.* I'd never been so happy to have an injury.

I went out to the living room, finding the apartment empty and not caring one little bit. I didn't give a shit where Luke was. I didn't care about anything. I had to get to that library and see if the book was real. I had to see what else might be down there.

I got onto the elevator and came out into the lobby. A group of employees filed towards me, everyone worriedly chatting away.

"Hey," said Luke, his face emerging from the crowd.

"Where's everyone coming from, a funeral?"

"Rook called an emergency staff meeting before he took off."

"Why wasn't I invited?" I asked.

"I tried waking you up, but you were dead to the world. I told Rook, and he said to let you rest."

I had the sneaky suspicion that Luke was lying. "I didn't see any invite."

He shrugged. "You should've seen a text on your phone last night."

My phone. Regular cell phones didn't work on the island, so they had their own set up. I'd been given a phone last week when I'd been a guest, but I hadn't seen the thing since before the storm.

"I don't have a phone," I said, wondering why Rook or Luke hadn't mentioned to get me one.

Easier to leave me out of staff meetings.

"Well, there you go," said Luke. "You can see Connie in tech support down in the offices and she'll take care of you."

I nodded. "Will do. So Rook left?"

"That's what the meeting was about. He wanted to go over the plan while he's away."

I found it surprising that his people looked so glum because of this. "When will he be back?"

"He didn't say, but he never does. Sometimes it's a month. Sometimes it's just days—but don't worry. We all know what to do. You won't be on your own."

I was sure he'd told everyone to keep a close eye on me, too. "I'm going for a walk. See you later."

"On that foot?"

"I'm fine. Just need to clear my head."

Luke gave me a disapproving look. "I'll be at the docks all day if you need anything. And don't forget to grab a cell from Connie."

"Got it." I watched him disappear inside and then I set out for Rook's cabin. Once there, I pushed on the door three times and hurried down to the library. I quickly went for the light switch, but nothing happened.

Shit. I hadn't come prepared with a flashlight.

I scrambled back to Rook's bedroom and opened the top drawer of his mahogany dresser. Next to a Bible was his flogger.

"Ah!" I pulled my hand away. My immediate response was to curse the violent thing, but it dawned on me that this sadistic tool enjoyed a level of intimacy with Rook that I didn't. It knew his darkest secrets.

Apprehensively, I sat on Rook's bed and picked the thing up by the leather-wrapped handle, threading the soft dangling strips through the center of my fist. The thing looked worn, like it had been used for decades. It even smelled like pain—salty and musty. For a fraction of a moment, I imagined punishing him with it, making him bleed for what he'd done, but the image instantly revolted me.

God, I'm so weak. It didn't matter what Rook did to me, I could never bring myself to feel any joy in watching him hurt like that.

I stared at the thing, my mind churning. Why was I so bothered by my lack of brutality? Maybe because I'd been told by the world my entire life to be strong and fearless. "Real girls kick ass!" But not all of us were built that way, I realized. Some of us were born with kinder souls. Some of us cried at the drop of a hat—during movies, listening to sad songs, or witnessing another human being in pain— not because we were weak, but because we loved so deeply. We cared too much.

It had always felt like a weakness to me, but sitting in this room, suddenly realizing this about myself, I didn't feel so weak anymore.

With a sigh, I placed the thing back in the drawer and went through the rest of the room. Truly, Rook didn't own much. A drawer of T-shirts. Another filled with boxer briefs and socks. Gliding my fingertips over his personal things made me want to see him again as just a man rather than the monster I'd built him up to be.

Finally, I got to the last drawer in the bottom of his dresser. I slid it open, my palms tingling as if my hands knew I'd find something. A giant maroon book sat on top of a stack of shirts. It was a thick photo album, the old-fashioned kind with little triangles glued inside to hold the corners of the pictures.

Once again, I sat on Rook's bed and turned the pages. Immediately, I recognized Rook. His gorgeous face, his tall body, was among a group of people lined up like an old high school class photo.

Weird. These pictures were in black and white, and I recognized a few faces. Luke, Mrs. Day, Dr. Rosy, and even some of the faces from the senior staff meeting. Frantic, I turned the pages faster. Year after year the photos looked newer until they went to color.

I went to the last page, which looked recent.

Shit. Everyone stood by the lagoon, lined up in

two rows. Rook in the middle.

I swallowed hard, got up, and put the album away.

Fucking hell. Rook might have lost his family as a boy, but he wasn't alone. They were all part of this place, and however it was being done, none of them had aged in at least sixty years.

CHAPTER ELEVEN

A search of Rook's library had not produced the book I'd seen in my dreams, so I could only assume it hadn't been real. But the album had been, as were the tens of thousands of records in the library that plunged deep underground, which was missing myself and Cici. God—or Rook—only knew why.

Add it to the goddamned list. Because I only knew enough to make me sound like a crazy person if I were ever to tell Warner. I had nothing solid on Rook or on how he managed to keep the island isolated from the modern world. I only knew *why* the island was special.

Yeah, but you're also missing the how. I would have to go through the library one more time.

Meanwhile, I decided to start documenting what I knew. Maybe it would provide clarity.

I went back to my room, got out my laptop, and began furiously typing. As random and crazy as the pieces were, I couldn't help thinking that the complete puzzle, the entire story, sat right in front of me. I just couldn't see it. Monks. Death. Living forever. Love. Sin. It all equated to this mess.

I released a deep sigh and noticed the time. I needed to get to the offices and meet up with the managers in charge of the fantasies next week. *I still have to focus on getting Rook to trust me.* I doubted there would be any other way out of this. Rook guarded his secrets carefully, and I was running out of time.

I entered the conference room, feeling more nervous than ever. Not because of me, but because of them. I knew their secret. First, there was Linda, the harem manager with short blonde hair. She looked my age. Douglas, the marine fantasy manager with straggly long brown hair, couldn't be older than nineteen. Craig, the bald black man with a beard, who handled anything historical, had flawless skin and looked thirty. And finally Paula, an Asian woman with heart-shaped lips who managed the smaller indoor sets, like the snowed-in cabin, appeared to be in her forties. Everyone looked like normal, healthy adults.

"Sorry I'm late," I said, taking the seat next to Douglas.

No one said a word, but they didn't have to for me to see they were upset.

"Is everything all right?"

Again no one spoke.

"Okay then," I said, unsure of what else to do, "let's get on with the meeting."

As each reviewed their checklists, I sat quietly, pretending to take notes. The tension in the air was palpable, but I couldn't begin to guess what had happened. Not knowing brought me right down to their dark moods.

"Oh, and I have your dates arranged," Craig added at the end of his report. "Jarod will be handling your cowboy fantasy—the Old West version—and Michael will be your Scotsman."

I felt the blood exit my face. "How'd you hear about that?"

"This is a small resort. Word travels quickly, and Rook also mentioned you'd be wanting to do a dry run. Your hosts are already cleared by Dr. Rosy, and Michael can see you at eight sharp tonight. Jarod at eleven in the morning, if you're up for it."

I raised a brow.

Linda chimed in, "Michael has a reputation for *leavin' the lasses a bit spent*," she said dryly, in a Scottish accent. "If you know what I mean."

I blushed. "Uh, thanks. I'll be sure to ask him to take it easy." But I couldn't do this now. Could I? Should I? Every time I had a plan or thought I knew what to do, something happened to shake the ground beneath my feet.

"Let me know how he does," said Craig. "Michael's really been working hard on his foreplay technique."

Linda grumbled, "Yeah, I hope so. Michael's nickname is the battle-ax. He sort of just goes right for it. Not a lot of tenderness."

"Oh." I nodded slowly. "Well, I guess some

women like that?"

"Not really," said Linda. "The *Outlander* fans are all about the romance."

"And the kilts," said Craig. "The dirtier the better."

Everyone agreed and began chatting among themselves. *Maybe a good time to probe.*

"By the way," I said, "I missed the meeting this morning. Did Rook say when he'd be back?"

The room fell silent and everyone's dark expressions returned, setting off alarm bells in my stomach.

Okay. "What?"

Douglas cleared his throat after a long awkward silence extending for a solid minute. "He didn't say, but he wasn't in a good—"

"Doug," Linda snapped, "it's not your place."

"Place for what?" I asked, tapping my pen on the notepad in front of me.

Doug shook his head toward his lap. "I think she should know."

"Maybe so," argued Linda, "but it's still not your place to tell her."

My heart flittered. "Tell me what?"

"Tell her," Craig said to Doug.

Douglas, with a mop of long brown hair and wide nose, looked at me. "Rook said he might not come back."

"What?" I dropped my pen, and it bounced off the table to the floor. "I mean—" I tried to gather myself "—he said he would be bringing back supplies for Dr. Rosy."

"Don't worry," said Doug. "He'll send all that stuff back on the plane, but he won't be on it."

Rook said he'd do anything to protect this place. He wouldn't just up and leave.

"Where'd he go?" I asked, knowing it was now pointless to hide my panic. Any idiot could see my flushed face and pale hands fisted into tight balls.

"He didn't say," replied Linda glumly, "but he told all of us to help you get up to speed as quickly as possible and that you would take the helm."

"Me?" I couldn't. I wouldn't.

"Why not you?" argued Doug. "He said you're perfect for the role—that you were born to do it."

What bullshit trick is this, Rook? He never let me get ahead of him. He kept knocking me out of place, always keeping me guessing.

They all stared expectantly.

"I have to go. I'm not feeling well." Nearly hyperventilating, I got up from the table and hobbled away.

"Should I tell Michael and Jarod you cancelled?" Craig called out.

I didn't reply and just kept on going.

Rook was gone. Gone gone. I couldn't begin to comprehend such a drastic move.

What would I do now?

Not wanting to insult Michael or Jarod, I put them off until the following week. I tried to pretend I could run an entire resort by myself—but really, I only had to assist the capable staff, who knew their roles.

Luke didn't find another apartment for me like he'd said. Instead, he moved out while I had been busy in the library, searching through guest records. I didn't want to feel snubbed, but I did. By him, by Rook, and by some of the staff who now treated me differently. I guessed because I'd been left in charge. The new girl. But luckily, the sting didn't last long. These past days alone had turned out to be an awakening, because I realized it wasn't a sin to care. It was only a sin not to. Somehow, I'd found strength in that, though I wondered if it would be enough to get me through.

It has to be.

There'd been no word from Rook, and I'd found nothing in his library apart from the guests' personal information for the past two hundred years.

Yeah. Two fucking hundred. Faced with that kind of information, I had two choices: believe that Rook and his crew had found the secret to cheating death, or believe it was all an elaborate hoax just for me. For the record, I didn't see why anyone would go to such lengths. In either case, while the information intrigued me, it solved zero problems. Not the Cici kind. Not the Warner kind. Not my kind.

By Monday morning, I had to face facts: only six days remained until I had to go home and answer to Warner. In the meantime, the plane rolled in and everyone took their places.

Fifteen women, ranging from twenty-eight to sixty-five, disembarked. For the first time since the hurricane, I saw the official guest greeter, Gerry, a huge Samoan man with tattoos on every part of his body save his face. The receptionists checked in the guests, the concierges got everyone settled, and the bellhops, kitchen staff, and housekeeping crew rushed with professional calm to attend to every clients' needs promptly. There were no VIPs and no Rook on welcome night, but it felt like business as usual, only the island felt stranger. The best and only way to describe it was that without Rook, the weird vibe of the island turned into a dark cloud. Everyone seemed on edge.

Still, I had no choice but to count my breaths and try to enjoy my final days before returning to New York. The fucking strange part was I didn't feel panicked anymore. Just the opposite. I felt quiet for the first time in a long time, like I'd finally made peace with it all. Rook had lied, Cici was gone, and I would never know why. This island made the impossible possible, and I would never know how. My life and all its turns had led me here, and I could be pissed off at the world for every "should have," but there was no point. My past was unchangeable.

After the welcome dinner, filled with some of

the happiest, rowdiest women I'd ever seen in my life, I took my place in the fantasy control room, schedule in hand, and settled in for a long night. The husband harem had been booked by four of the fifteen guests, which meant they'd be running fantasies almost every night.

I grabbed a coffee from the break room and sat in front of the screen as a plump mature woman entered the tent. The men lined up, naked, and the harem master helped her select the order.

I can't say I'd ever seen anything so illicit, but after the first two men had sex with her, I felt numb to it. Anesthetized. I began watching the subtle things—the way the men touched her, whether or not they made eye contact and for how long, the pace of their hips. Not before long, I found myself talking quietly into my headset, coaching the men to slow down or give her more attention. A few guys had glanced into the camera—hidden above—and winked at me, like we were all part of some secret pleasure team.

By guy number five, I began yawning uncontrollably. There was no passion in this, no love. Just two bodies satisfying physical need.

I flipped open the folder in front of me, containing the woman's profile. I assumed Mrs. Day had screened her because I hadn't. There'd been no time.

Selena Colbeck was fifty-four years old and from Ohio. She had three children, all grown and done with college. Her husband, Frank, owned a construction business and worked up to seventy hours a week. During her check-in with her personal concierge, Selena had said that as hard as she tried, as much as she'd given, her husband and children had never shown her any real appreciation.

"They make me feel invisible. They think that clothes magically appear clean and folded in their drawers. Dinner shows up on the table. The car drives itself to soccer, baseball, and swimming. In all my years, I can't recall any of them saying a heartfelt and genuine thank you. For once in my life, I want to know what it feels like to be seen. I want to be waited on and adored. I can't live my entire life not knowing what that's like."

How fucked up is that? I thought. But Selena's words made me realize that this was more than sex in her eyes. She needed to fill a giant lifelong void. Maybe after this—getting a taste of being worshipped—she might go home and change her life. *Or demand her family treats her better.*

After two hours, Selena was limp and sleepy and had only really been with about six of the men. She fell asleep on the silky soft bed and the rest of the "unused" hosts left. The ones who'd slept with her stayed. It was about the strangest thing I'd ever seen, watching six chiseled men all curling up on an enormous bed around this woman who looked like she just might die of happiness right then and there.

I went to sleep that night alone in my bed with

a smile on my face for the first time in months. I never dreamed that helping a woman fulfill her fantasy could be so fulfilling to me. But it was.

Maybe Rook's Island does have a purpose.

CHAPTER TWELVE

The week passed uneventfully and by Sunday morning, we had a plane full of happy faces returning stateside. I discovered that Sundays were for the employees. Everyone gathered in the late afternoon near the dinner club and nearby dock for food, music, and relaxation. Because we were so many, the people flowed outside and sat on lawn chairs they'd grabbed from the pool or on picnic blankets.

It was kind of nice, really. The staff worked around the clock for six days, giving fifteen women a slice of heaven, and then they let their own hair down.

As for their drab moods, I still sensed a strong undercurrent of worry—why wouldn't they be concerned about Rook abandoning us?—but maybe after the stressful week, people just needed a moment to forget. I know I did.

I grabbed a Corona from the cooler just outside the dinner club and took a sip. The hunky hosts, most of them shirtless, so they could "work on their tans," as one guy said in passing, mingled with the housekeeping crew. The phone operators chatted with the concierges. I didn't see any cliques or pecking order.

Just one big family. Did they all know that this island was some sort of fountain of youth?

"Stephanie, how was your week?" asked a deep voice. To my disappointment, it wasn't Rook. *Luke.*

Standing on the edge of a patch of grass, I smiled at Luke, who I now knew wasn't in his forties.

"Good, actually. Really good," I said, playing it cool.

His brows twitched. "You're serious."

"Sure. Why wouldn't I be?"

"I took you more for a city girl who needs her traffic and lattes."

"Me?" I laughed.

"Well, yeah. I mean, you've been nothing but stressed out since you got here."

Thinking about a homecoming with Warner Price will do that to you.

I took a sip of my frosty beer, just perfect to cut the heat of a warm October day. "I guess you're right. But I'm good now." *Just trying to come to grips with death—something you know nothing about.*

"I'm glad to hear it, then," Luke said. "I felt kind of bad leaving you on your—"

"Stephanie?" A huge man with long red hair and beefy arms came up on my right. His was a face I'd seen via a monitor.

"Michael, it's nice to finally meet you.

Clothed." I extended my hand, and he gave it a quick shake. "I've only seen you naked or in a kilt, but you do board shorts pretty well." I cracked a smile, hoping a little humor would avoid any awkwardness.

By the pissy look on his face, I don't think it worked.

"Are you sure that you're 'pleased to meet me'?" he asked. "You didn't even speak to me once this week."

I frowned for a moment, mulling. "Oh. You mean coaching." I had seen him working his ass off, pun intended, but I'd been so absorbed in observing the women, I'd barely noticed him.

"You did an excellent job. I only saw very happy faces," I said.

"Really?"

"Yeah. Really," I said.

Michael's expression immediately warmed, and he stepped in closer. "Then why did you cancel on me twice?" he whispered.

I'd been booked for my own personal tour of the Scottish Highlander fantasy, but I'd been too busy. *Don't lie. You wouldn't have done it anyway,* I told myself.

"I-I'm sorry. Don't take it personally. It was my first week and—"

"Well, I'm free tonight. And I'd love to show you the castle." He chuckled in a deep, baritone voice. "Or perhaps you'd like to go for a midnight swim."

Luke practically lunged at Michael. "Not funny," he snarled at Michael, who was about twice his size in the muscle department.

I opened my mouth to say something, but Luke wedged himself between us. "Move along now," he said to Michael. "She and I were talking, and I don't remember inviting you to the conversation."

Michael threw back his head of flaming long red hair and laughed. "What are you, her brother? Oh, wait." He grinned sadistically, not backing down. "I know. I heard you tried to get her in bed when you were living together, but she turned you down. That's why you moved out, right?"

Luke placed his hand on Michael's chest, pushing him back. "You know nothing. So fuck off."

"Luke?" I grabbed his arm. "Don't you have some oxygen tanks to check on?"

Luke snarled at me with those hazel eyes.

"It's fine," I pleaded with Luke, not wanting the two of them to go at it. Besides, why was he acting so protective? It was more than chivalry. He didn't want Michael and me even speaking.

Luke gave Michael a long, menacing look. "Watch yourself." He walked away to go hang out with Team Pirate and the yoga instructor gal I'd yet to formally meet.

"Fucking Luke. Always thinks he's the boss," Michael groused.

"Something like that," I said, not really meaning

it.

"So you wanna go for a private tour of the castle? It's one of the oldest structures on the island." He leaned in. "And it's full of secrets. I hear you like those."

"Heard from who?"

"Word gets around. So you interested?" He wiggled his coppery brows and held out his large hand.

He had my attention, though I doubted anything he could show me would make one lick of difference at this stage. Still, I was in no position to pass up the opportunity to learn another of Rook's secrets.

"Sounds great." I took Michael's hand, feeling Luke's eyes on me.

The moment we passed the threshold of the torch-lit entrance of the castle, I instantly felt the air shift around me. It was cold, dark, and smelled like moss and dankness. I knew this was part of the effects, but my skin still chilled and my cold lungs couldn't tell the difference.

"It's kind of amazing," I said. "So real." The torches mounted to the wall gave us little light, but it was sufficient to see the level of detail in the stonework and the intricacy of the thick woven tapestries hanging on the wall.

"Been to Scotland, have yeh?" Michael said with a thick brogue.

"No. But the castle is exactly what I imagine it would be like."

"I hear that a lot, ye kin?"

I shook my head. "Okay. You can stop with the accent."

"Neah, lass. Yeh must give yur self to the High-lander way. 'Tis a thing of beauty."

I crinkled my nose. "I got a C in high school drama. I was never good at pretending."

"They all say that, lass, until," he pushed open two large wooden doors, "they see this."

"Wow." It was an enormous room with a cav-ernous ceiling, several plush red sofas, an antler chandelier, and a fireplace big enough to smoke an ox. Furs lined the floor of the dimly lit room, and the sound of rain pelted the beautiful stained-glass windows. Sound effects.

"'Tis jus you an' me on our weddin' night, lass."

They really knew how to set a mood, but I wasn't about to lie down in front of that fireplace with a strange man.

"Stephanie, lass? You look so beautiful standin' there." He stretched out his hand. "But you'd look even better wrapped in mi arms."

Michael was a nice-looking man with a very nice body, but when it came to lust, I'd only ever felt it for one man. Ironic, really, because, as Rook had said, he was the one thing on this island I couldn't have, and part of me still wanted him. I knew it was just as wrong as it was irrational, but what did it matter now? Rook was gone.

"How about that tour?" I urged. "You mentioned the castle has secrets."

"Aye." My Scot in board shorts stepped forward and wrapped his thick arms around my waist. "But I'll hafta be takin' off mi pants to show ye."

Ugh. I should've known. He knew nothing, or if he did, he wasn't going to share it. Luke probably scared him off.

I pushed back, and he released me. "I'm sorry, Michael. I can't."

"Why not?"

What could I say? "Would it make any sense if I told you that I'm not a fantasy type of girl?"

He dropped the accent. "So you are a hypocrite."

"Sorry?"

"You don't want to lower yourself to our standards. You think we're all dirty for what we do."

"What? No. I just don't think I'll ever be the sort of person who can detach my body from the rest of me. And the rest of me only wants something real. I can't jump into bed and feel comfortable or turned on by a man I don't really love."

Michael grinned, like he'd won some bizarre prize. "So you're sure you don't want to fuck?"

"No. And, for the record, I don't look down on what you do." If anything, this week had given me a new appreciation for how hard they all worked to make the fantasies about more than simple sex. "I'm just built differently."

Michael nodded, looking happier than hell.

"What?" I snapped.

"Rook was right about you," he said. "You are a good person. And we are all lucky to have you here protecting us. Now," he bowed his head, "if you don't mind, I have some beer drinking to do. Today is my cheat day."

He left me there in front of the crackling fire.

All right. That was weird. Then it dawned on me. The staff thought I'd be filling Rook's shoes and looking after them. The person who'd come here with the intention of ruining it all. *And I have to leave tomorrow.* A supply plane had just flown in about an hour ago, and I planned to be on it, heading stateside in the morning.

"What am I going to do?" I whispered to myself and walked over to the plush, velvety red sofa by the fireplace. I plunked down.

"Hello, Stephanie." Rook's deep voice sliced through the darkness.

My lids sprang wide open. "Rook?"

He stepped from the shadow of the doorway, wearing a black suit. Though the room was dimly lit, I could see he had a thick growth of short black whiskers.

"You're back." How long had he been standing there?

"Indeed, I am," he said coldly and strolled over. "Not a moment too soon, I see." He grabbed my hand and yanked me to my feet. "What were you doing with him?" he snarled.

Too stunned to protest or push away, I simply stood there in awe. I hadn't realized how much I'd missed his beautiful face or the delicious scent of his skin.

"Well?"

Rook was upset, but I wasn't sure I cared. *He's here. He's back.*

"We were just talking," I muttered up at him, my heart thumping away like a rapid drum. "Where did you go? Tell me why you left," I demanded quietly.

His pale eyes drilled down on me, and his grip tightened on my shoulders. I could feel the anger radiating from every pore in his body.

"To tell her I couldn't fucking do it anymore," he growled. "To tell her I tried, and I fought, but I can't fucking do it one more day."

Slowly, I shook my head from side to side. "I don't understand."

"I renounced my vows."

Whatthefuck? "What do you mean?"

"Exactly what I said."

My immediate reaction was to laugh. This was another classic Rook move in his never-ending game of mind fuck.

"What is it you find so funny?" he asked, his

pale blue-gray eyes filled with intense emotion bordering on rage.

"Wait. You're serious."

"I have lived my entire life protecting this island, praying for the people who belong to it. And I've never asked for anything but their safety. But since you came here, the only thing I can think about is you. You're like a goddamned fever I can't rid myself of."

I blinked, my mind racing to fully grasp his words.

He continued, "And believe me, I tried to get you to leave. I tested you in every way possible, hoping you might prove me wrong, because it would make my life infinitely easier. But at every turn, you only confirmed what I already knew."

Like a giant lightbulb flickered on, I saw the picture clearly. *It was all planned.*

I gasped. "'Tested.' You mean like leaving me alone to run the island or making Luke my roommate."

"That was part of it, yes. I needed to be sure you weren't here for the wrong reasons or easily tempted."

"But I..." My head started to spin. All along, I'd assumed that Rook was just playing a mean game of chess because he saw me as the enemy, when really it had been some elaborate setup.

I didn't know whether to be pissed or...or...I didn't know, really.

He took my hand. "I understand this hasn't been easy for you, especially trusting me when I made sure you had no reason to. But I had to know if your feelings were real, if you would be loyal to me no matter how difficult."

Difficult. Now there was a word that grossly understated what I'd been through since coming to the island.

Against every urge in my body telling me to get closer, I gently pushed away from him and took a seat. I'd heard him say words like trust and test and loyal. But there couldn't be any of that between us. Not until I knew for sure what had happened.

I looked up at Rook, who remained standing. "Tell me the truth, Rook. Did Cici really drown?" *Don't you dare look away from me. Please don't.* It would mean he was about to lie.

"Yes." He held his gaze to my eyes, and my heart opened up just a little wider.

"Then why didn't you look for her? Why lie to me about it?"

"Who told you that? It is untrue," he said, outrage in his voice.

"It doesn't matter who. Just answer the question. Why didn't your staff hear about her death or help look for her?"

Rook held his irate gaze to mine. "By the time she was reported missing, it had been six hours," he argued. "The current could have carried her in a hundred different directions over a thousand square miles. No one here would be of any use, which was why I called in favors from the Bahaman Coast Guard. But I told you this already. All of it. As for telling the staff, I was far too busy firing our entire security team to have discussions with every single person on the entire island. So I do not know who knows what, nor do I care. My job is to make sure those responsible were removed from my island and to ensure it never happens again."

I folded my hands neatly in my lap and stared at them. I could keep pushing and doubting and fighting, but all of a sudden, I couldn't see a reason to do so. I wanted to believe Rook, and his response had seemed genuine.

He took a seat beside me and grabbed my hand. "Stephanie," he said softly, "there is something I need to tell you."

I looked at him and held my breath.

"No matter how sorry I feel for the grief I've caused you," he said, "and the shame I feel over not having done more while she was under my care, I selfishly cannot regret knowing you. In all my years, in the millions of breaths I've drawn, not one made me feel alive until your arrival."

I couldn't breathe. The dark weight festering inside had simply evaporated. It jarred me right down to my bones. I'd been living like this for months—grieving, fighting, hoping—but just like that, it was all over.

"So you're not a monk anymore," I said, "and

now you're asking me to do what?"

"To be with me."

My insides fluttered out of control while our eyes remained locked on each other. *Goddammit, he's so beautiful.* And the way he made me feel was like nothing I'd ever known. A sense of fate or rightness mixed with passion.

I swallowed down the lump of nerves in my throat. I knew I was about to take a giant leap, because there were still so many unanswered questions, but like him, I couldn't fight it anymore.

"Yes," I whispered.

He leaned in and kissed me hard, his strong hands cupping my cheeks.

I kissed him back and began pulling at the front of his shirt, tearing buttons and frantically loosening his tie. He quickly shrugged off his coat and shirt and then lifted my shirt. He said nothing, but the carnal look in his eyes was pure hunger. For me.

Lucky him. Because I'd never felt so fucking in need of giving myself.

Rook pulled me down to the floor onto the furs. In front of the fireplace, we kissed, grabbed, and panted like beasts.

Rook's mouth broke away, and his lips trailed down my neck and collarbone. His hand cupped my right breast while his mouth covered my left nipple. I felt him hard and ready against my thigh, which sent my body off a cliff. The hollow, fluttering ache between my legs became a scorching need.

"I think the last three weeks count as foreplay," I panted.

He smiled up at me and those two deep divots puckered in his cheeks. "But it's my first time. I want to savor it."

My breath stuck in my throat. "Fuck, you're so sexy." A man like Rook knew everything there was to know about sex—he'd seen it all. He had a keen sense of what women wanted. But now, it was my turn to show him what he'd been missing.

I rolled him over and straddled his body, letting him play with my heavy breasts. His eyes stayed glued to them as he ran his thumbs over my tight nipples, and I rocked my hips gently over his shaft, which was still covered by his pants. He groaned deeply, but I didn't want him to spend himself like that. Not this time.

I moved to the side, getting on my knees, and unbuckled his belt. Staring into his fiery eyes, I unzipped his pants and reached inside. His long, thick cock felt tight and hot in my hand as I stroked the velvety flesh.

His eyes fluttered shut, and he groaned. That was a sound I'd never grow tired of. Sexual, animalistic, hungry.

I bent my head and kissed the head, circling my tongue over the ridge of the crown. He tasted like male, musky and sinful.

As the scent of his pheromones flooded my bloodstream, a rush of violent desire charged through me. I wanted this man in me, on me, touching every inch of my skin.

I opened my lips completely and enveloped his cock in the heat of my mouth.

He grunted and bucked his hips.

"God, this is what I have been missing?" he whispered with a gruff tone.

I took him deeper, stroking him with my lips and tongue until I felt his strong hands on the back of my head. He was close. So damned close, but I wouldn't let him come. Not yet.

I pulled away, wiped my mouth with the back of my hand, and got rid of his pants completely. I stood and let him watch me remove the last barrier of clothing.

"You're so beautiful, Stephanie. Do you know how many nights I've dreamed of taking you, how hard it was to resist not fucking you when you were naked in my arms?"

I knew because I felt the same.

I lowered myself, kneeling beside him once again, trailing my fingertip from his collarbone between his chiseled pecs and over the hard ridges of his ripped abs. His smooth, tight olive skin seemed like it had been poured over the muscles. "I won't ever get tired of looking at you." I sighed, wanting to remember the feel of him underneath my fingertips.

I ran my hand to his shaft, which stood almost straight up. It twitched as I glided my fingers over the textured silky skin.

"What are you doing besides trying to drive me mad?" he asked.

"Making sure I never forget." I glanced at him. "It's my first time, too."

He frowned in question.

"I've never been with a man who made me feel like this," I explained.

He sat up and gripped me by the shoulders, opening his mouth to say something. Instead he kissed me with scorching emotion.

He suddenly pushed me down into the furs and rolled on top of me, nestling himself between my thighs.

I opened my eyes, knowing what would come next and wanting to recall every second.

Rook stared into my eyes. "Thank God. He finally listened to my prayers."

I brushed wild strands of black hair from his forehead. "What did you pray for?"

"You." He thrust with his hips, driving deep. I threw back my head, gasping with pleasure and digging my fingernails into his shoulders. He withdrew and drove into me again. For as long as I lived, I would never forget the feel of his hot, steely flesh filling me, the soft head pressing into the entrance of my womb, begging for his cum.

As our hips rocked and ground in unison, pushing and coaxing the flames higher, the only thing I could think of was that Rook was inside me, and our bodies felt so right. A thousand fantasies with a thousand men could never come close to this. Whatever connection existed between us couldn't be faked.

Our mouths kissed with hunger, our bodies shook with need, our hearts thundered with desperation.

I slid my hands behind his neck and sealed our mouths tightly. He slid his hands under my ass and drove deeper.

"Oh God." I felt it coming despite never wanting this to end.

"Fucking hell." Rook threw back his head and pushed forward with his hips, triggering a soul-shattering orgasm deep inside my core. It roared through my breasts and stomach, arms, legs, and toes.

My teeth clenched. My body froze. The waves of delicious shocks charged through me. I cried out, my walls contracting around his pulsing erection ejaculating deep inside me.

Several mind-blowing moments passed before I could draw air again.

"Fuck." I relaxed my entire body, melting into the soft furs. "Was that really your first time?"

"Why?"

"Because you'll only get better and my heart can't take it."

Still inside me, Rook bent his head and kissed me softly. "I'll try to work you up to it."

CHAPTER THIRTEEN

After administering several long lazy kisses, Rook withdrew slowly, and I closed my eyes, enjoying the euphoria of my limp muscles and heated skin damp with sweat—his and mine.

Rook stretched out beside me, and his hand slid down my chest, resting on my lower stomach.

A long silent moment passed, and I opened my eyes to see his face.

He's staring at my stomach. "What are you doing?" I asked with a big fat smile on my lips.

"Imagining."

"Care to elaborate?"

He made a little circle underneath my navel. "No."

But the look in his cool eyes couldn't be mistaken for anything other than, well, longing.

The lightbulb flickered on. *Whatthewhoa.*

"You're not thinking what I think you're thinking," I said.

Rook gave me a condescending look, as if to say *Of course I am. Don't be naïve.*

"I-I think we just, and I am not read—"

"You didn't ask me to use a condom, and you're not on birth control, are you?"

"No. But…"

"But what?" he said sternly. "I've waited my entire life for you, and we both know this is more than a fling."

I didn't know anything other than I felt something powerful between us. "Rook, I—"

"Are you denying it's what you want?" He sounded bitter. "Because I want you. More than anything, so I plan on fucking you at least three more times tonight and coming in you every chance I get, which will only lead to one place. Why bullshit around the subject?"

Clearly, Rook was from another time and had very different expectations. Nevertheless, we'd had sex a mere few minutes ago, and he was already jumping to babies.

My heart jittered inside my chest. To say I was freaking out would be a giant freakin' understatement.

I stood and started dressing, careful not to put too much pressure on my foot.

"Where are you going, Stephanie?" He stood, too, and crossed his arms over his bare chest.

"I'm feeling a little overwhelmed right now. I, uh…this was…" I shook my head.

"I asked you a question." He grabbed my arm and yanked me back.

"Hey, let me go."

He released me. "Do you have any idea of what I've just given up for you, of the sacrifice I just made?"

"No. That's the problem. You haven't told me anything, but you expect me to—"

"Two hundred and thirty," he blurted out.

"Sorry?" I blinked.

"My age. I am two hundred and thirty years old."

I stepped back.

"Do not act surprised. I know you found my home, my real home. I know you went through my things. I know you saw the albums and the library."

Still naked, Rook stepped closer, refusing to give me space, and gripped my shoulders. "I thought you understood."

I shook my head. "Not everything. Not how."

"There is no explanation, Stephanie. But not everything in this world is meant to have one."

"What is this place?"

"The fountain of youth. But you already knew that."

I did, but nonetheless, hearing it confirmed sent an ugly tremor right through my stomach. "Like in the legends?"

"Nothing like the legends—not even close."

I had nothing to say to that.

"Come," he said. "It's time to show you everything."

⌒ ⌒

Rook dressed, and we went to his real home. Not at all surprising, there were two entrances. One inside his hovel, and another fifty yards away, hidden inside a stone shed.

"You did not honestly believe that I climbed out of a dirt hole every morning?" he asked.

Now that he mentioned it, I guess that would make it hard to keep his suits nice and clean.

"I was too busy with all your other mysteries to give it much thought," I said.

"Well, this is the easier way down. You are always welcome." He tapped on the door to the shed, and it popped open just like the other one. Inside was a narrow wrought-iron stairwell that led straight into his bedroom. The door was behind the big beveled mirror.

"After I show you this," he said, "there will be no secrets left between us."

I couldn't lie, I felt nervous. He'd already confessed some pretty shocking news—his age. *To think, there's more...*

He went over to his closet and opened the door. Behind the fine suits was yet another hidden door.

"This way." He went on ahead.

This was the moment I'd been waiting for. No, not waiting. Fighting. It almost felt too good to be true. After so many games and lies, part of me still couldn't let go completely. And that part still clung to suspicion. Would I ever trust him completely?

I wanted to. I really did.

"Coming?" his deep voice called out.

Cautiously, I stepped inside the bright room filled with old books, knowing exactly what this was. "Your real library." As I said the words, my eyes gravitated toward one big book in front of us on the top shelf. It had a red butterfly on the spine.

It's the one I saw in my dreams. I walked straight to it and plucked it off the shelf.

"See. You do know." Now dressed in just his slacks and a white dress shirt with a few buttons missing at the top, he crossed his thick arms and leaned against the doorway.

"I saw this book in my sleep. How's that possible?" I thumbed through the pages. It was exactly the same.

"I cannot say, but it seems you have a special connection to this place, as do I. As does everyone who's ever come and swum in the lagoon since the massacre."

I stared up at him. "You mean the monks that were murdered. The ones you witnessed."

"My family owned a sugar plantation in Jamaica, and after my mother died of a fever, my father fell in love with one of the farmhands. She was originally from Martinique."

"You mean she was his slave."

Rook nodded. "Yes. And he married her anyway. He said he didn't care what anyone thought because in the eyes of our maker we were all equal. He believed that his faith would protect us, too, but that didn't happen. The other families in the community came after my father, my stepmother, her sisters, and anyone else related to either family. They burned our home and crops, killed my new baby brother, and slaughtered anyone in the fields. We barely escaped with our lives on a small boat."

Jesus. How sad. I would never understand the brutality of men.

Rook went on, "When we landed here on Friar's Island, we knew we'd found paradise. The monks who lived here had been persecuted for centuries by one religious group or another. They welcomed us. We worked by their sides. The senior monk, Father Rook, treated me like his own grandson. He taught me to read and write in five different languages. He told me their stories and taught me their beliefs. But when I grew older, I began to see that Father Rook was much more than a monk. He could heal people. He could sense what others felt. He had been touched by God, and when those men came, they killed him. They killed my family save my aunt, who they left for dead after brutally attacking her."

I covered my mouth, horrified by his story. "They left you alive, too."

Rook stared at the wall, his brows knitted together. "I think they were the sort of men who killed and took for pleasure. They saw no pleasure in killing me, so they didn't. Instead, they made me watch as they slit my father and stepmother's throats. They killed my older brother. They saved Father Rook for last."

I held my breath, vividly watching every horrific moment unfold in my mind. "What did they want?"

"I don't know, really. They talked of hidden gold, but there was nothing apart from the food we grew and each other."

"Did they know about the lagoon?"

Rook looked at me with intense eyes. "I swam in that lagoon a hundred times. It wasn't until after the event that I noticed something different, when I found my aunt face up on the muddy shore of the lagoon, completely unscathed. Not only that, she appeared younger. But I saw what they'd done to her before they tossed her in the water right after they killed Father Rook. The water saved her. And only her."

"How's that possible?"

"Who's to say? But I remember as they held the knife to Father Rook's throat, he looked at me and made me promise to carry on his work. I vowed I would, and I believe that whatever gift Father Rook had inside him, he left it behind. For me."

I'd never heard anything so outlandish, but the proof stood right inside this room.

Rook continued, "It was very difficult for my aunt and me after that. But my promise to Father Rook gave me purpose. My aunt saw her survival as a divine intervention. We moved on. Years later, groups of foreigners began showing up, mostly men from the other islands, who wanted to claim it as their own. I knew I had to do something, but without money, my aunt and I were sitting ducks. We had no weapons. No men of our own. No means to protect this place or each other."

He drew a deep breath and exhaled mournfully. I knew it couldn't be easy telling me all this. If I were in his shoes, I'd be in tears by now.

He went on, "That is when my aunt came up with the idea to use the only asset we had: the lagoon. So we began visiting nearby islands and bringing people back with us for a fee. Soon word traveled and made it nearly impossible to sell our service openly. People would mob us, screaming for the miracle we carried. We knew then we'd have to be more careful and selective. We took the bit of money we had and bought guns, lumber, and hired a few men we felt would mind their own business, and began building the first version of the resort. I assumed my role as the wealthy, eccentric man who owned the island. My aunt began quietly promoting our natural healing retreat to the wealthy. We built what you see today carefully and quietly." He looked at me with those sharp, piercing eyes, waiting for a response. My guess is he wondered if I believed him.

"I need to sit." I left the room and went over to his bed, taking a seat on the edge. This was a lot to take in, and though I understood what he believed, I wasn't like him. I didn't have faith or believe in God, let alone miracles.

Regardless, I had to admit, "It's amazing," I muttered. "Everything you've been through. Everything you've done."

Rook came and sat next to me. "It was done out of necessity, and now it's over."

"Why?" I asked.

"I have broken my vow, and whatever connection I had to Father Rook's gift went with it; though, I knew this would be the case. A man can't turn his back on something so powerful without consequences. The consequence is that without the fountain of youth, we cannot maintain the island's independence. It costs millions to pay off everyone who protects us from annexation."

Now I understood. At least, I understood a big part of it. "Isn't there another way, like invite more guests? This is a beautiful island."

He placed a large hand on my leg. "Stephanie, what I did not tell you is that the effects of the lagoon do not last for an eternity. It brings one to their perfect state of youth and health, but it doesn't stop the ravages of time. You begin aging all over again, and the more times you've used it, the faster the effects wear off."

My heart dropped into my stomach. "How many times have you used it?"

"Too many."

Fuck. Oh fuck. "How long do you have?"

"I do not know, but whatever time I'm given, I would like to spend it with you."

"That's the reason you want to rush into it with me." But how unfair. Did he think about me? "You can't seriously want to just make me love you and then leave."

He gave me a harsh look. "Place yourself in my shoes. If you had given your entire life, decades upon decades and then some, granting wishes to others while being shackled to a life you chose simply for survival, wouldn't you want a piece of your life all to yourself? To love the person you were meant to be with?" He drew a breath. "I know what I'm asking is selfish, Stephanie. But I have made thousands of people's dreams come to life. I deserve to have mine too. And it is you."

My eyes teared with emotion. "So this was your plan all along," I whispered.

"I tested you—I watched—I saw how you connected with this place and with me. Once I was sure about you, after you insisted on staying, I knew what I wanted. I knew I had to rescind my vows. It is why my aunt and I fought before she left. It is why I went to see her to ask for her forgiveness. She will age, too."

The weight of Rook's decision finally struck home. He had broken his vow, the lagoon would no longer rejuvenate, the island would lack the money to fend for itself. *He's going to die. All for a short time together.* He had pawned it all just for me.

My heart swelled with sorrow. Because now I knew that this thing between us was real, so real that he'd given everything for it.

He continued, "Understandably, my aunt is not ready to die nor let this island go. Not after everything we've given to keep it."

"How do you feel?"

"People are not meant to live for eternity." He rubbed his bristly chin. "And after I am gone, life will go on. So will yours. And if I am very, very lucky, you will give me an heir to carry on a piece of who I am."

No. No. He doesn't understand what he's asking me to do. With all my might I tried not to cry. This was too much.

Rook placed his hand over my heart. "I love you, Stephanie. I have from the first night we danced and I held you close. I knew you were special, and I knew you came here for a reason."

"I came looking for Cici." I stared down at the floor, not wanting to look at him.

"But you stayed for me, didn't you?" He grabbed my chin gently and tilted my head, forcing me to meet his gaze.

I had told myself that I stayed for revenge and for Cici. Now, I knew that wasn't true. I had stayed for this.

Fucking hell. Every word he spoke made me want to love him in the most tragic, inescapable, and epic way.

"I can't say I regret meeting you," I said. "I just

wish you and I had happened some other way. And I wish it didn't mean that your life…" I couldn't say the words.

He brushed a lock of my dark hair behind my ear. "I'm ready for it to be over, Stephanie. I'm ready to have my time with you, loving you every moment of every day." He kissed me hard, and I melted into him, his sweet taste and delicious scent. I melted into his warmth. But then the resistance came. My heart bucked like a wild horse battling captivity. Rook wanted me to love him with everything I had. And then watch him die. Maybe with his child inside me. What woman in her sane mind would sign up for that plan? I had already endured so much—the loss of my mother, my father's mental abandonment, my sister drowning—but this? He wanted me to knowingly journey to a place so dark and agonizing that I might never recover.

"I-I don't think I can do it, Rook."

He returned his large warm hand to my leg and gave it a soft pat. "It's a lot to ask. I realize this. And I am sorry for not telling you earlier, before we made love. My eagerness is a reflection of my desire for you. Just promise you will think about it."

"I will." I bobbed my head. "I promise."

"But do not take too long, Stephanie. The clock is ticking." He kissed my hand and stood. "I leave you to reflect, but know that it is all or nothing. If you stay, you commit to me and a life together, no matter how short. You stay with me until the very end." He turned, heading for the door.

"Where are you going?" I asked, my eyes wet with gut-wrenching conflict.

"I must start making preparations—the staff will need to be resettled."

"What about the ones who've been with you a long time?" I wondered if they would age rapidly, too.

"I spoke to them before finding you in the castle."

"And?"

"I think they saw this coming. But they know they will be cared for during what remains of their time."

I didn't think that my soul could possibly weigh any heavier, but as Rook left the room and I realized that it wasn't just his aunt and himself who would age and die, but all of the people in those photos, too, I lost it.

Rook had made the decision to leave behind his monastic life for me and the dream of us—even if for a short time—but I felt like this was my fault. If I'd never come here, if I'd left during the hurricane evacuation, if I'd done one small thing differently, maybe none of this would have happened. Of course, I knew in my heart that it wasn't so black and white. Every step of the way, I had taken the only path available, all of it starting with Cici.

I drew a breath, facing yet another crossroad— grant my beautiful Mr. Rook his one fantasy or walk away.

CHAPTER FOURTEEN

That night, I stayed in Rook's bedroom—his real bedroom—and went through the bookshelves in his hidden library. I read through the historical records of the island, the ones in English, anyway. The books spoke of the monks who had settled here, seeking refuge from persecution due to their radical beliefs—mostly tied to the "crazy" idea that all men and women were equal in the eyes of God. Not a very popular point of view during their time, which ended with their massacre in the 1790s.

To add to their tragedy, had those monks not been murdered, they would've lived to see slavery abolished in the early and mid-1800s. Of course, the monks had been fighting and dying for centuries, long before their massacre, and the journey to equal rights for all wouldn't end with abolition. Still, the world had changed because of people like them, and they never got to see it.

Sitting at Rook's desk in his room, I closed the book and blew out a long breath. I knew the world was filled with things that couldn't be explained, but I wasn't able to make the mental leap and accept that a real-life fountain of youth existed, born out of a tragedy. Yet I'd seen the proof with my own eyes when Rook aged ten years and then suddenly looked younger in the space of one day.

How is this possible?

It didn't really matter now. If Rook was right, and I had no reason to doubt him, this miracle's time had come to an end. He was the link that tied whatever was in that lagoon to this world, and now that connection had been severed.

I lay back in his soft king-sized bed covered in white linens, and smelled his pillow. His scent was unlike any man's—like he bathed in pure sugar and leather and oranges. Add some chocolate and he'd be the perfect treat. My mouth literally watered for him.

But then I remembered the not-so-sweet part to all this: I'd be losing him.

My heart started pounding like a war drum in my chest, going all crazy. I felt like my body would explode.

Breathe, Stephanie. Breathe.

I closed my eyes and tried to think of something else. Something calming. I drifted off, imagining Rook and I walking on the beach, hand in hand, and laughing about something trivial. But there was nothing ordinary about the way we looked at each other. It was like we were exactly where we were meant to be, living a beautiful, ordinary life filled with love, family, and the sorts of silly problems a person begged for.

రా ళా

"Stephanie?" whispered Rook's masculine voice, followed by a lingering kiss. "It is time for you to wake."

My eyes fluttered open to find a set of sparkling blue and silver eyes watching me intently.

"You're so beautiful." I sighed.

"And so are you." He kissed me again, hovering for a long moment. "Sleep well?"

"I dreamed of you."

"Then very well, indeed." He smiled softly.

"Mmmm…" I groaned and stretched my arms, feeling the warming effects of Rook's proximity.

"Please do not make that noise unless you want me to fuck you again. There's only so much torture a man can take." He grinned, showing me those adorable dimples in his still unshaved cheeks.

Hearing him say the word *fuck* instantly made me think of just that. Him, riding me hard, pumping his tight ass.

"The look in your face," he said, in a baritone voice, "tells me you don't think it's such a bad idea."

"I don't. It's all of the other stuff that scares me." His growing old and withering away right before my eyes. "How much time do you have?" I whispered, subconsciously trying to memorize every detail of his face.

Wearing a white T-shirt and navy linen pants, he stood, his expression turning stone cold. I now knew that was what he did when he wanted to hide his emotions. The poker face.

"Why don't we put our attention on something else?" he suggested.

"Such as?" I sat up in his bed.

"Something I need to tell you."

"Okaaay?" He sounded way too serious. I didn't like it.

"I am leaving the island to you, although I am unsure of its future."

"You're leaving it to me."

Rook nodded. "Yes. It may no longer have its main attraction, but it still has a lot to offer. I also assume the Bahaman government will attempt to annex you and wish you to pay taxes, enforce immigration laws, etc."

"Um, I don't know what to say. Can we…maybe just not talk about estate planning just yet?" Everything was moving way too fast. I still hadn't wrapped my head around Rook's age.

"Of course. I understand. We'll save all that for another day."

"Thank you." I exhaled.

He took my hand and kissed the top. "In that case, since today I am a free man, what would you like to do?"

"I'm not sure. What did you have in mind?" Given his situation, I imagined he had a long list of things he'd been deprived of.

Rook cocked one dark silky brow. "Aside from fucking you?"

Crap. How long would I be able to resist him? The way he looked at me made my core roar with need. The way his tall, well-constructed frame took up room made my skin flush. The way he made me feel so desperate to love him, despite knowing it wouldn't last, made my soul ache. I wouldn't be able to hold out.

I suddenly thought of last night. The way our bodies had moved together and the sound of his deep voice when he came. Then I remembered him placing his hand on my stomach afterwards.

This is fucked up. I can't do it. I can't.

I jerked my hand from his, attempting to keep my wits in check. "I can't stay and watch you die. I can't let you get me pregnant and leave me all alone to raise a child."

Rook took a long moment before responding while his jaw flexed. He didn't look happy, but he didn't look angry either. "I admit, I had hoped you'd give my proposal more than one night of consideration—"

"I don't need more time. I know I can't handle this."

"Stephanie, you will be well looked after either way."

He thinks that's the problem? "That's very generous, Rook. But I don't want your money. I don't want to live my life missing you. I don't want to have your baby."

"You might already be pregnant."

My stomach rolled, and the blood drained from my face. He was right. It only took one time, and frankly, I was in the middle of my cycle. I'd known it last night. I'd known when he'd been coming inside me. I just hadn't cared. No, that was the wrong way to say it. I had cared. About him and me and what our bodies wanted: To be together. I'd wanted him with everything inside me at the deepest emotional level. Then everything had changed the moment he'd told me the hard truth: he and I would never grow old together. We'd be doing it apart.

I lifted my chin to meet his stern gaze. "I'll cross that road when I get there."

"Promise me that if you get there and find you are pregnant, you won't do anything to change course."

I blinked at him. *What a horrible conversation.* Why were we even having it? I could only come up with one explanation: He didn't want to waste time.

"Rook, how long do you have?"

He looked away.

I jumped from the bed and stuck my finger in his face. "No! You tell me the fucking truth. How long?"

The vein on the side of his neck pulsed, but he wouldn't look at me.

"Rook, so help me God, if you don't start coming clean, I will leave. To. Day. You will die without another word from me."

His head whipped in my direction. "You play a cruel game of hardball, Miss Fitzgerald."

"The last time I checked, expecting honesty from someone you love isn't hardball. It's just what you do."

He stared for a long moment, his right eye twitching. "You love me." Not a question, but a reaffirmation.

I nodded.

"Why?" he asked sharply.

"Because you're not afraid to sacrifice yourself—your soul, your life, your beliefs—to help others get to a better place in life."

He gave me a nod.

"What the hell does that mean?" I snapped. Who responded with a nod when a woman proclaimed her love?

"It means it's a good reason. I accept it." He smiled mischievously.

"You're a bad man, Mr. Rook." I huffed.

He shrugged. "Perhaps."

I leaned into his warm body and wrapped my arms around his neck. "Not perhaps. Most definitely."

He brushed back the rebellious brown locks of my hair. "Do you really love me?"

I wanted to crack a joke or say something witty—affection and soul baring wasn't my forte—but I couldn't make myself go there.

"I do, Rook. I really do."

"Then in that case, please call me James."

CHAPTER FIFTEEN

James had refused to tell me how long he had left to live, and that only meant one thing: not long. But did that equate to days, weeks, or months? I couldn't hope for years. Because after I'd gone back to my apartment to take a shower and dress, James and I met outside. It was almost noon, the sun high in the sky, and the streaks of silver on his temples had doubled in width. The lines around the edges of his serene eyes and gorgeous lips had deepened.

My heart fell through my feet, burrowing deep underground, seeking protection. It didn't want to open its eyes or face this pain. It begged me to shield it from the torment. Still, I forced myself not to act selfishly. I couldn't fall apart every time I saw evidence of this impossible situation.

"Hi." I went to my tiptoes, placing a soft kiss on his stubbled cheek, and then ran my fingers through his soft, silver hair. "The look suits you."

"Thank you." He dipped his head. "Just wait until I am completely silver. You'll never want a dark-haired man again."

"It's like they say, once you go gray, you never

stray."

He frowned. "That, Miss Fitzgerald, is the worst joke I have ever heard. And I have heard many."

"I'm sure you have. By the way, you do realize you're a giant pervert for sleeping with me, right? I mean you're old. Like, dinosaur, petrified sap, oil reserve kind of old."

"Ah, but with age comes wisdom." He bent his head and kissed the soft spot at the base of my neck. "And I know many, many things."

I knew he was an expert when it came to what women desired, and after last night's sampling, my body hummed with anticipation.

"I dunno…" I sang teasingly. "You were kind of a letdown. Reminded me of amateur hour."

His jaw dropped. "You are a cruel, cruel little beast."

I smiled playfully. "I am. But thankfully, you're too old to catch me." I smacked his chest and turned to run, quickly remembering that I wasn't so fast on my feet either. "Ouch!" I gripped my foot. "Motherfucker!" The stitches teared or something.

James chuckled halfheartedly, quickly scooping me into his strong arms. "Too old, my ass." He laughed. "Let's take you to see Rosy."

I beamed up at him, feeling like I was being carried by an invincible giant. "You're good at being the hero, James."

He frowned for a moment, like he didn't appreciate my compliment, but then smiled ahead. "It's a monk thing. We enjoy martyring ourselves for the sake of others."

I bobbed in his arms as he carried me along the gravel path, his feet crunching beneath us.

"Well, you're good at it," I said. "And most importantly, you look fucking hot while you do it."

"It's the robe. Women have a thing for devoutly religious men."

Only when they look like hot underwear models. Honestly, Dave Gandy came in at distant second compared to James.

"But are you really that devout?" He didn't live the most sanctimonious of lives.

"Yes, though I'm certain my faith would be shunned by ninety-nine percent of the people on this earth who subscribe to the usual religions."

"Why?" I asked.

"If I were to list every reason, it might take the entire winter, spring, and summer."

We didn't have that much time, which crushed my soul.

"Then in a nutshell?" I urged, trying to keep my mood as light as possible. It wouldn't serve either of us if I started blubbering.

"One might call us the original hippies."

I laughed. "Oh boy, now you've turned me on. Please tell me you don't bathe and own a year's supply of patchouli."

"Hardly." He frowned. "But we do believe in your standard free will and that one's purpose must always be driven by love and the greater good—and all that godly gracious mumbo jumbo."

"Mumbo jumbo. Is that like hocus-pocus, and if yes, sign me up."

James gave me a stern look.

"Sorry. I didn't mean to diminish your beliefs. I just never understood why so many people pray to a God who clearly isn't there."

"How do you know?"

Where did I start? Because if he or she existed, why would God permit so many children to suffer, James having been one of them? Why would men rape women? Why would God allow people to strap bombs on their bodies and blow up a school full of little girls just for wanting an education?

"Like you said," I replied, "it would take an entire winter, spring, and summer to explain."

"All right then," James said. "You may believe in a godless world, and I may believe that there is more to life than what you see with your eyes and touch with your hands."

"Such as?"

"Miracles," he replied. "They happen every day. And for some, every day for over two centuries."

I narrowed my eyes at him. "I see where you're going with this, but there could be a scientific reason for why the lagoon made you young." Some unique combination of chemicals in the soil and water. Or maybe there was a very particular magnetic anomaly. After all, we weren't so far from the

Bermuda Triangle.

"There very well could be; however, I choose to believe otherwise. Either way, I will die, and it will remain a mystery to me." He looked at me with warm eyes. "But that is the beauty of the human condition. I have my own mind and I am free to believe whatever I choose, and so are you. Yet no matter where we come from, no matter our age, gender or race, we are still capable of love, and its existence is rarely argued by any sane person."

Love. He believed that it tied us all together. It was strangely endearing and romantic. And how James managed to come across as a strong, intimidating man while he spoke about such a sensitive topic was yet one more mystery.

"You really are like the world's oldest hippie," I said jokingly.

"But better dressed." He grinned, and I swear I could feel my heart peeking out its head from that dark, dreary cave just to smile at him and bask for a few precious moments in his light.

"I can't argue with that."

"Such a shame, because I love it when you do," he joked.

"Ha. Funny." I smacked his strong shoulder.

Still holding me in his arms, he took the path that headed north. "Humor is another of my many hidden traits."

"Can't wait to find out what the others are. In the meantime, what are we doing for the rest of the day?"

"A very good question."

"Then answer it." I couldn't wait to hear what the master of fantasies had dreamed of doing all these years while watching thousands act out their deepest desires.

"You know that I want to spend the day making love to you," he replied. "However, as you're not entirely on board with the strings attached, then I can only think of one other thing I'd like to do."

The mere thought of those strings made the space between my legs pulse. Physically, all I wanted was for him to bend me over and have his way with me. Mentally, I wanted to run from all this because my heart couldn't handle the pain of losing him.

"All right. So what is second on your list, then?" I waited.

"I would like to murder the men on that ship who killed my family."

The air left my lungs with a sharp exhale. "Huh?"

"Aside from wanting to find a woman I can love with all of my heart and have children with her, the only other thing I've ever desired was to make them suffer."

"You aren't joking," I muttered.

"No. I am not."

I tried to keep my expression even, but likely looked horrified, which was likely why he lowered me to my feet right beneath a giant cedar tree.

"Do not judge me, Stephanie. You of all people should understand the rage, the hate, the need for justice after losing your sister."

"I do, but—"

"But what? Am I supposed to be above all that simply because I believe in God? Do you expect me to be a better man than you are a woman?"

"Nuh-no. It's just…you're a monk."

"*Was* a monk. I am no longer bound to the vows I took to find forgiveness in my heart for all manners of sins. And given that I could never forget what I witnessed that day as a child, I've had to beat myself for over two hundred years. Do you have any idea what that is like?"

Shamefully, I looked down at my feet. "I don't." I knew what it was like to lose my mother and sister, but I never had to atone for my feelings.

"Well, imagine how I felt, remembering those men brutally beating and raping my aunt—a healer, a lovingly kind woman who only sought a life of peace."

I couldn't imagine. I wouldn't.

He continued, "My days may be numbered, but I would like to offer these men the same kindness they showed my family. I would like, for once in my life, not to turn the other cheek."

But James had told me that he'd watched those assholes die in the biggest storm ever to hit the island. He said he'd watched their ship sink to the bottom of the ocean only a mile north.

"They're long gone, James. Can't you just let it go?" I grabbed his arm.

The nostrils of his perfectly straight nose flared. "I lied in order to hide the effects of the lagoon."

I whooshed out a slow breath that inflated my cheeks. "Please don't tell me they're alive."

"Six made it to shore. My aunt and I were able to subdue them one by one."

"And your aunt didn't kill them?"

"She believed it would cost us both our souls." James looked at me. "Stephanie, I am not a wicked, sadistic, or brutal man. I have never stabbed a woman while I raped her in front of a ten-year-old child. I would never kill a person in hopes that they might confess to owning a mound of gold that only exists in legends—"

"But you would make them swim in that water and keep them alive for centuries in hopes that someday you might be in a position to make them pay."

He nodded. "You understand me completely."

I didn't know what to think exactly. "It's not right."

"Imagine Cici hadn't drowned. Imagine Cici was my aunt and that a man stabbed her womb while she carried a child."

Jesus. "Whose child?"

"Does it matter?" he asked.

I shook my head no. "But I'm still asking."

"Father Rook's. He renounced his vows only

days before he died so he could marry her—a long-standing tradition to carry on the sect. But he never got that chance, and I was the one who had to watch my aunt deliver her stillborn child. I had to bury the baby that would've eventually taken Father Rook's place."

"I don't think I want to hear anymore." I felt sick. Literally sick.

"So now you see, Stephanie, to suffer in prison for such a heinous crime doesn't suffice. Nor can I, in good conscience, free them. And since the island's fate is unknown and my future is short, I cannot risk them getting out. It is incumbent upon me to do what is right."

To my shock, I couldn't argue. Perhaps these men eventually felt bad about their actions, but that wouldn't be enough. Not to me. Because I wasn't a person who believed that every sin could be redeemed. Some people were just bad, plain and simple. So given the chance to let them live, just hoping they might be cured or change, I wouldn't do that for one simple reason: I wouldn't be the person who paid the price if I was wrong.

When I was five, we had a dog—a mutt we'd adopted at the pound. She was medium sized with brindle markings on her legs and the softest black ears. When we played, she would wag her long black tail and lick my face until I nearly peed in my pants laughing. As far as dogs and kids go, we were best friends. But when Milly bit my sister, Cici, for getting too near me, and then bit the neighbor's one-year-old in the hand after Milly escaped from the yard, my dad told us that Milly had to be put down. Even Cici cried. We begged for him to find another way and, to his credit, he tried. He hired a trainer. He bought drugs to calm her. We did everything, but a few months later, Cici went to pet Milly's shiny black tail and ended up with six stitches in her arm.

"Please don't kill her, Daddy," I'd cried.

"It's my fault! I scared her," Cici screamed.

"Someday, when you have your own children, you'll understand," my father said.

"Just chain her up in the yard," I begged.

"Baby," my father said, "that is no life for Milly, and if she ever escapes, she will hurt someone. But not a grown-up. She's smart. She only bites the ones she knows aren't a threat to her. Small children."

I didn't understand. Until now. Sometimes, we had to do what was right for the greater good. Even if it meant killing. Because if we simply kicked the can down the road, eventually someone else would pay. And men like these were just like Milly in that they only prayed on the vulnerable. Unarmed monks, women, and children. James's father. Easy targets.

Still, why would James want to die with this on his conscience? He believed in heaven and hell, I assumed. And monk or no monk, he still believed in his god.

"Just leave them with me," I said.

James looked at me like I'd lost my mind.

"I'm serious," I said. "I don't want this on your conscience, and I'm sure I'm capable of making sure they stay imprisoned until they grow old and die."

For the first time ever, James looked conflicted. "I will think on the matter."

"Don't think about it too long," I said, mirroring his comment to me yesterday.

James didn't reply, but took me to see Dr. Rosy, who checked out my foot, redid my stitches, and taped it up nice and tight. She said I needed to use crutches, and if I ripped them again, she would be forced to chain me to the gurney. The gleam in her eyes told me she meant it, too.

James waited outside as I hobbled from the building.

"This does not look promising," he said.

I smiled at him, feeling a sense of immediate longing. I couldn't see him and not want more.

"Nor does that look in your eyes," he added.

"Sorry. It's just—"

"Intense," he guessed.

I nodded.

"Well, since you cannot walk, and we have had enough of emotional topics for one day, I think I have the perfect solution. Something to ease the burdens of the day."

"Is this number three on your list?"

"No. This is something I enjoy doing at least

twice a week."

"Oh, an activity on the monk-approved list." I hoped it wasn't praying or meditating. I was in no mood for self-reflection or quiet time. "Is it making beer?"

He chuckled. "No. I am not a Trappist, and this is something even you cannot find fault with."

CHAPTER SIXTEEN

"Oh, hell no. I am not getting on that—that thing."

"It is called a horse, Stephanie. And her name is Maria. Her bloodline has been on this island for almost as long as me." James patted her shiny black coat. "She is my pride and joy."

The mare turned her head and attempted to nibble on James's white T-shirt.

"Mr. Rook, I wondered when you'd show up." A man emerged from the barn. He had stunning sky blue eyes, tanned skin, and honey blond hair. It was Jerod, the resident cowboy. I'd seen him on the monitors, but in real life, he was much more spectacular. *No wonder he's on the top ten favorite fantasy list.*

"Miss Fitzgerald, it's a pleasure to meet you," he said with a twang.

"Jerod, nice to finally meet you in person." I held out my hand, balancing myself on the crutches by wedging them between my arms and body.

"Yes, ma'am." He shook my hand, and I immediately noticed his rough leathery palms.

"Wow. You really are a real live cowboy," I said.

He dipped his head. "Born and raised on a Texas cattle ranch." He winked.

"How did you end up here?" I asked.

He looked at James, who nodded. "It's all right. I have told her," James said.

"About time," Jerod replied.

I still couldn't believe that James had orchestrated everything just to test me. I supposed I had suspected it all along. Nevertheless, it all felt surreal.

Jerod returned his attention to me. "I was a Texas Ranger, reporting to Samuel H. Walker."

"I'm sorry. I don't know who that is," I said.

"The co-inventor of the Colt revolver. I fought for Walker in the Mexican-American War," Jerod said proudly. "We were captured by the Mexican army on April 28, 1846, during the Thornton Affair. The ones who survived the ambush were taken prisoner and later exchanged, but three of us escaped before that. We made our way to the Gulf of Mexico, stole a boat, and planned to get back to our side, but a storm carried us off, and I washed up here."

"Jerod was nearly dead when I found him on the beach," James said.

"So you saved him," I guessed.

James nodded. "He's been with us ever since."

"That's amazing." Even more so, Jerod looked to be twenty-five, tops.

"It's been a good life." He patted James on the arm. "I ain't got no complaints. Except if you don't take Maria here out for her daily ride. She's been yammering all mornin'."

"I wasn't aware that horses yammered." I grinned.

James chimed in. "Like you, she doesn't quit until she gets what she wants. And neither do I." James slid his arms around my waist and pulled me in close. "So it's either this or we go back to number one on my list."

"Fa-fa-fine," I stammered, knowing I was too close to giving in and making a decision I'd only regret later. "I'll ride her."

James released me. "Such a shame. For I long to ride something else altogether."

I frowned. "I opened the door and walked right into that one, didn't I?"

"Yep," Jerod smirked. "Ya sure did."

"Let us get the horses saddled. You may wait here," said James, chuckling his way to the barn.

Jerod stared at me for a moment, studying my face.

"What?" I asked.

He shrugged. "I get it."

"Get what?" I asked.

"When Mr. Rook got us all together to break the news last night, I thought he'd gotten kicked in the head by Maria. But cha know what? I get it. A man can't live on bread and water alone."

The guilt inside caused me to look at my feet. "I'm sorry."

"I sure the hell ain't. It's a blessing to wake up every day doin' whatcha love and helpin' people." He held up his rough palm. "Now, I git that some folks might think I've lived the life of a sinner, but I know in my heart that the world is a better place because I chose to love and not kill. James showed me the way."

The more passionate his speech, the thicker his twang. It was charming, actually.

"So now that you won't be able to renew your lease, so to speak, how do you feel?"

He shrugged again. "I always knew it couldn't last forever. Not when the cost is so high. It's never sat well with me." He scratched the back of his head. "But yanno what, Miss Fitz? That Mr. Rook has been like a father, brother, and best friend. I couldn' ask for more."

I crinkled my nose. My brain hung up on the word *cost*. Really, James's entire family had to die in order for that lagoon to do what it did, but that wasn't what he seemed to be talking about. He'd said "is" and not "was."

"Yeah. The cost. How have you managed to live with it?" I asked, fishing.

"I guess it all goes back to the day I signed up for the Rangers. I knew the risk and it was mine alone to take. I wudda kicked anyone who tried to talk me out of it. So I guess it's the same thing. Let each man, or woman, make their own choices."

Whatthewhoa? We weren't talking about James's

family being slaughtered. So then what price did he refer to?

Before I could ask, he dipped his head. "If you don't mind, I'll see what's keeping Mr. Rook." He turned and walked away.

Less than a minute later, I heard heated rumbles erupt from inside the barn. I stepped closer, trying to listen in, but my crutches and clumsy steps made it impossible to sneak up.

"Ah, Stephanie," said James, emerging with Maria in a shiny brown saddle, "your mare is ready." He held out his hands and then laced his fingers together. "Are you ready?"

I nodded yes, though in that moment, it dawned on me: Something still didn't feel right.

"You have been awfully quiet," said James as we strolled along the beach on our horses, the sun high in the sky and the afternoon breeze whipping through our hair. James's horse was a tall white stallion named Tony. My horse, Maria, kept trying to go her own way, in the direction of any leafy plants.

"Just enjoying the view." I gazed out over the calm turquoise waters.

"How is your foot?" he asked.

"Fine." I left my bad foot dangling from the stirrup, which seemed fine as long as the horse didn't bolt.

"Let's not play games, Stephanie. I overheard your conversation with Jerod."

"Oh?"

"Yes. And I am very disappointed that you still seem suspicious after everything I've told you."

James pulled his horse to my left, but I didn't look at him. Instead, I continued gazing to my right, out over the never-ending stretch of ocean.

"Dammit, woman. If you have something to ask, then ask. But I don't have time for this bull-shit."

Woman. Huh. I swiveled my head in his direction. "Then maybe you should come clean and tell me everything."

"I have."

I hissed out a breath and shook my head. "Yeah, like you had sex with me and then told me you're dying. You mean like that?"

James looked down at his hands gripping the reins, looking completely at home on his horse. "That was not how I'd planned on things going. But understand, Stephanie, the need to be with you was—*is* overwhelming. So, yes, I should've told you what was happening first, but I am still just a man—flawed and apparently very susceptible to my feelings for you, the woman I've been waiting my entire existence for."

If that wasn't romantic, I didn't know what was. And I couldn't lie, his words speared me right through the heart. Nevertheless, James was right. A part of me still didn't trust him. Maybe I never would, but who could blame me? He was a man cloaked in secrets, and I'd known it the moment I laid eyes on his gorgeous face.

Searching for my words, I listened to the crash of the small waves hitting the beach. "All right." I looked at him. "What's the price you pay for the lagoon, James?" If he looked away, then I'd know he was lying.

But James wasn't looking at me to begin with. He held his gaze on the stretch of beach ahead. "The price is different for everyone, I suppose. Some find that restarting one's life anew isn't as easy as they'd thought."

"In what way?"

"To begin, you must cut ties with everyone you know—close family, children, friends. But I believe the biggest price is living on while they do not."

"So the price is missing them?"

"I can't speak for everyone, but yes. This is generally the biggest challenge. Which is why I always spend time with my VIP guests, preparing them for a journey that may extend their lives by sixty to seventy years. Afterwards, I make visits to check on their welfare or they come to the island. I am here for them until the very end—if they need someone."

"So when you say 'until the very end,' do you watch them…"

"Die. Yes, if they need someone."

"Why?" I asked. "I mean, that's kind, but isn't it hard?"

"The guests who've swum in the lagoon over the many centuries may have paid a lot of money, but they remained alive because of me and the choices I've made around this island. I feel responsible for them until their time is up." He gave me a look. "And no one should ever die alone or afraid."

Given his childhood, I could understand why Rook, I mean James, didn't like to see people afraid in their final moments. "So you're there for them."

He nodded.

"And before they go, how did you get them to keep it all a secret?" I would think that eventually, the guest, or anyone who'd swum, might tell a friend or something.

"I really have no way of verifying that they do; however, we've managed to remain in the shadows of the world for over two centuries."

"So then how do you find the VIP clients?" I asked. Because James had been charging one million dollars to take a swim, and not a lot of people had that kind of money sitting around.

"Obviously, the island itself and the resort are not entirely a secret. Some guests come to us for our standard package and it is clear they are not in good health. We do background checks, find out if they are worthy of living another life, then we offer them the service if we think they can afford it. Not everyone qualifies, however. One must have lived an exemplary life dedicated to something noble."

"Such as?" I asked.

"Raising children, caring for others, fighting for a better world in their jobs—there are many ways."

I nodded, thinking that through. "Women only?"

James smiled. "No. Not women only, but because of our fantasy services, few men pass through. Most of them start as employees. After five years, we must decide if they are candidates or we must let them go."

"Because they'll notice some of you aren't aging."

"Yes, but you will not have to worry about any of that, Stephanie. After I am gone, you will run the island free of this burden. No secrets."

After he is gone. The idea made my soul feel heavy and dark. "I never said I wanted to run this place, let alone own it."

"Why?"

"Because everything here reminds me of you. And Cici. I just wouldn't be able to deal with that."

"Ah. I see." James nodded pensively. "Well, speaking as someone who has more than one lifetime of memories, some not so beautiful, I can tell you that it does get easier. The pain dulls. And perhaps, at some point, you might find the memories of the ones you've lost to be comforting."

I shrugged. I couldn't imagine being comforted when right now everything felt raw.

"So, have I convinced you?" James asked.

"About what?"

"To let go and trust me?"

I wanted to. Really I did. "There's just one more thing I want to know."

"Yes?"

"How long?" I asked.

James's jaw tensed. "If I tell you, it will only make it more difficult. You'll be staring at the clock, thinking about a point in the future instead of spending each moment with me. Here. Now."

"I understand that."

"And you still want to know?" he asked.

I nodded. "Yes."

He looked ahead. "About seventy years ago, I met a woman—a guest who came to us with a very unique fantasy." James glanced at me with a subtle hardness in his eyes. "She had been a prisoner in a concentration camp during World War II and lost everyone."

I felt my skin crawling with dread. I could only imagine what a person in her situation might want. Revenge. Justice. To erase the horrors stuck in her mind.

James continued, "She wanted to see her entire family one last time. She wanted to hug them and tell them that she loved them."

"That's all? She didn't want to make those people pay for killing them?"

"No. She simply wanted to surround herself

with the love of her family—her husband, children, and parents—one final time." James's expression turned icier. He wanted to hide his emotions.

"Were you able to give her that wish?" I asked.

"We were not equipped at the time. But after she left, I fell into a dark place. Here was a woman who had endured the unthinkable, and her idea of paradise was being surrounded by her family. Her children. I realized that my life was hollow and always would be because of my obligations to Father Rook and this island."

"So why didn't you quit?"

"I did. I gave up. I stopped swimming in the lagoon. I resolved to die. It took less than a month before I was too weak to leave my bed."

A month. Only a month. What the hell? That was not enough. I needed more! My heart began thumping out of control. "What changed?"

James glimpsed at me. "You."

"Me?"

"The thought of you. As I lay there preparing to let go, I saw this flash—this image of me walking with a woman, holding her hand. We were laughing and talking, but there was this ease about us. It was happiness."

Christ. Exactly like the dream I'd had last night of the two of us. But how?

James continued, "And I knew that when the time was right, when it was meant to be, I would meet this woman. I would not die never knowing what it is like to love another person so deeply and passionately."

I fell speechless. How could we have the same dream?

"At the time," he added, "I could not see her face, Stephanie. But the moment I saw you, I knew. I knew it was you I'd been waiting for."

I forced myself to continue looking at him while my heart and soul spiraled like a powerful tornado inside my body. How could I ignore it any longer? I felt what he felt. I felt that connection. And as painful as it would be to lose him, it would be more painful living the rest of my life having turned my back on him.

I pulled back on the reins to stop my horse, so he did the same.

"Stephanie," he said, "I tell you this story because it answers your question about how much time we have. But I hope you will also see that it doesn't matter. I would have given it all up for merely one day, one hour, one minute of being loved by you."

My eyes teared, knowing that what came next wouldn't be easy. "Yes."

"Yes, what?"

"Yes. I accept your proposal. I will stay with you until the end."

James dismounted and then grabbed my arm, sliding me off my horse and easing me to the ground. "Say it again."

"Yes."

"Excellent. Because the question was 'Will you marry me?'"

"You're not serious," I said.

"I am. And you've already said yes. You can't take it back." His grin stretched from ear to ear, making it nearly impossible to push back.

"We don't have much time, and I'm not sure I want to spend it planning a—"

"This is Rook's Island," he argued. "We are prepared to make any fantasy come to life in a matter of hours."

At this point, marrying him would be symbolic. I'd already agreed to stay by his side and watch him meet his maker. It was insane, irrational, and frightening. But it was what my heart wanted and that made it all feel right.

"Yes. We can marry," I said.

James dipped his head and placed a soft kiss on the side of my mouth, threading his strong hands through my loose hair. "I love you, Stephanie." He kissed the other side. "I love you."

"I love you, too."

He covered my mouth with his, and the kiss was anything but gentle. His lips were demanding, his body language filled with hunger.

He slid his arms around my waist and pulled me tightly into his frame, allowing me to feel the hardness between his legs.

I let out a muted moan. His taste, the feel of his

warm body, the sweetness of his breath created a vacuum in my mind. All I could feel was my need for him. Nothing else.

He broke the kiss and turned to grab the pack on the back of his horse. "Here." He pushed it into my hands. "You carry this, and I will carry you." I took the pack, and he scooped me into his arms, heading inland.

"Where are we going?" I asked.

"You will see."

He carried me through the lush jungle along the path for several minutes. Then the trail turned into a sharp incline, but James barely broke a sweat.

"You're really strong for such an old man," I said, smiling.

I could see the happy gleam in his eyes, and I had to admit, nothing felt better.

"Just wait until we reach the top. I'm going to show you how strong when I fuck you senseless."

My body exploded with heat, thinking of the way he'd taken me last night. I couldn't begin to articulate how sensual he'd been.

Once we got to the end of the path, James gently put me down. There was a small cliff below us, butting up against the beach. And with the slight elevation, we could see the endless array of colors, ranging from deep turquoise blue to an iridescent green, of the Atlantic.

"Wow," I said, the warm wind whipping against my face. "This view is amazing."

"I won't argue." He gazed at me hungrily.

I would never get enough of this man. Not of those lips. Not of those pale blue-gray eyes. Not of that smile or how I felt when we were together.

James laid down a gray blanket and placed the small basket to the side.

"You really are *the man*—perfect location, perfect view, perfect romantic words."

"Perfect woman at his side," he added.

"That was corny, but a good one." I hobbled over, closing the gap between us. "Kiss me."

He tilted his head to one side and tucked a lock of my long dark hair behind my ear, but he didn't kiss me.

"What's wrong?" I asked.

"I changed my mind. I am definitely not going to fuck you. I'm going to make love to you. Slowly."

My mind turned into a swirling mess as his head plunged and his lips pressed to mine. I opened my mouth to him, allowing his tongue to slide and dance with my own. I couldn't recall ever being kissed like this before, not even by James himself. Every stroke of his tongue, every kneading movement of his lips, had his heart and soul poured into it. This was what it felt like to be given a kiss from a man who loved you with everything he had.

Oh God, I don't want to lose him. But I couldn't afford to think like that. I had to force myself to stay present and to drink in every delicious moment.

I let my fingertips float over the round firm

mounds of his chest and down to his stomach before latching on to the hem of his T-shirt.

I pulled up and removed his shirt, quickly returning to his mouth and kisses. I could sense the desperation in him now, the consuming need to join our bodies. I felt it, too.

I removed my own shirt and lay down on the blanket. He kneeled and slid my shorts off along with my panties before doing away with the rest of his clothes.

James stretched out by my side, tilting the length of his body toward me, pressing his erection into my hip. His hand then began stroking and wandered slowly while I lay there watching, brushing my fingers through his soft hair, enjoying the feel of his warm skin pressed to mine.

No one had ever touched me like this and made me feel so utterly consumed by them. I tried not to think about missing this after I watched him grow old in a matter of weeks. I couldn't allow myself to go there.

James placed his hand between my legs and began gently massaging my throbbing bud. My breath caught and then escaped with a hard whoosh. He began kissing his way down my collarbone, my breasts, my stomach, each kiss bringing him lower. My body tensed in anticipation.

I glanced down and James smiled up at me, a devilish look in his beautiful nearly translucent eyes. Not breaking eye contact, he placed a kiss over my aching c-spot. I threw back my head and grabbed fistfuls of blanket. He flicked his tongue and ran it up and down over the sensitive skin, then down to my already aching entrance.

I moaned softly. My nipples turned to hard points; my arms and legs trembled with ecstasy.

"I love touching your body, Stephanie. I love the way you taste. I love the sound of your voice."

"Then don't stop," I panted, wanting more.

He kissed his way up my stomach, leaving a trail of sensual tingles, and laid himself between my legs. The head of his rock-hard shaft nudged at my ready entrance.

"Tell me now if you don't want this," he said, staring intensely. "I know I'm asking for a lot."

He was asking for the impossible—my love, my commitment, and my consent to let him try to get me pregnant. But I couldn't walk away. I think maybe I knew it from the moment I arrived on the island.

"I said yes, and I meant it. But don't think I'm going to give up hoping for another miracle: you living a long happy life with me."

"You can't spend your days wishing for something that will never happen, Stephanie. I am here now. You are here now. You have to make that enough."

My eyes teared. I didn't want to cry in front of him; it didn't seem right to let him watch me suffer.

"I'll try," I said solemnly.

He kissed me slowly and then pushed his hips forward, sliding his cock deep inside. His heat radiated into me, through me, igniting so much more than my sexual arousal. Still, I savored the feel of his hard velvety shaft gliding in and out, the weight of his body, the sound of his breathing as our kisses became more feverish.

I opened my legs wider, needing more of him, to get him closer. He felt so right. With our rhythmic movements, I lost track of time, of the blue sky above, of the jewel-colored ocean below. I forgot where we were or when. There was only him, me, our bodies moving together.

After what felt like hours, his pace quickened, and I felt my body climb toward a release that would break me into a thousand pieces when it hit. I rocked my hips faster and dug my fingertips into the firm mounds of his ass, coaxing him to fuck me harder.

His pace turned to a ravenous hammering, and then James let out a deep, masculine sound somewhere between a roar and growl. His hips pushed hard, driving his cock as far as it could go, triggering an explosion inside me. My walls contracted around him, milking his cock for every drop of cum. I moaned so loudly I could hardly recognize the sound coming from my own mouth.

"Ohgod," I panted. "Please don't stop."

As the orgasm raged through my body like a wild fire of euphoria, bright lights clouded James's handsome face. I fell instantly transfixed by his surreal beauty—the swollen full lips, the proud cheekbones, the sharp angle of his jaw. But more than anything, it was how I felt inside in this moment.

After several long breaths, James opened his eyes and beamed at me, the sunlight catching the browns and bit of red in his dark strands of hair. I studied him, my mind high from what our bodies had just done.

I sighed. "I never noticed that your eyes have so many flecks of silver, like a million sparkles."

He kissed me softly. "They've gotten lighter with age."

"Why?" I asked, my voice above a whisper.

"Maybe the eyes really are the windows to the soul."

"So what do your windows say?"

"That I am a complicated man." He grinned.

That he was.

I drew a slow breath. "I love you."

"And I love you. Time will never change that."

I looked at him, committing his expression to memory. So much love for me. I ran my fingers over the side of his graying temple, and my smile faded. The patch was bigger now. Even over the last hour.

The end was already beginning.

CHAPTER SEVENTEEN

"Do you really have to go?" I asked, standing in the doorway of my apartment, not wanting to waste one moment of our time together.

James cupped my cheek with a rough hand. "Yes. But I will meet you at the dinner club at eight."

"Why there?"

"We are having a little farewell party for those who are…not part of the club, so to speak. They must leave before they begin to notice the changes in the longtime employees."

My heart wept. "I can't go to that," I protested quietly.

"Why not?"

"Aren't they mad about losing their jobs?"

He laughed. "No. They're all being compensated quite well."

"What about the ones who aren't leaving?" We hadn't actually seen many people today, but we'd come across Linda and Douglas. They had given me looks. Maybe they hated me. Maybe they didn't understand what Rook saw in me. *Maybe they're just trying to accept it all like you are.*

James studied me for a moment. "You feel that you've done something wrong."

"No. I mean yes. I'm the reason it's all coming to an end."

James bowed his head and kissed me softly on the cheek. "You are the reason I am free. And not everyone has swum more than once—some still have a long life ahead. As for the others, the ones who've been with me a long time, they have had wonderful lives. They are not afraid of it ending."

"I wish I could feel the same."

"Nothing lasts forever, Stephanie." He pulled me into his strong frame and held me tight.

"I know, but I don't have to like it."

"I understand how you feel," he said beneath his breath, and kissed me again, his tongue sweeping across my bottom lip.

My body rapidly heated for him, craving the rush and ecstasy only he could deliver.

I hooked my finger around the waistband of his pants and tugged him closer. "Please stay." I slid my hands to his ass and squeezed.

"Mmmm…maybe I do not have to leave so quickly." He reached behind him and shut the door.

I beamed up at those hypnotic eyes. The way he looked at me with absolute adoration was intoxicating. He made me feel loved and desired and safe.

I quickly pulled up his shirt and unbuttoned his pants, sliding them all the way down to his ankles.

His cock was ready for me, the soft skin tight around the hard, thick length of him.

He stepped out of his pants and moved toward me, reaching for my shirt. Within seconds I joined his nudity and we were going at it in my living room, our bodies pressed tightly together, my hands clawing and stroking every inch of his hard body I could manage to reach without leaving his lips.

James leaned into me, forcing me back until my ass met the armchair. He suddenly broke away and spun me around, pressing his hand between my shoulder blades.

My heart pounded against my rib cage, knowing what he meant to do.

I braced myself on the top of the chair's back, fully bent over, offering myself to him.

"Fucking hell, I can't take it. You're so sexy." He slid his hands between my legs, stroking my wetness, spreading it over my throbbing bud.

I jolted with pleasure, my breathing erratic.

"Tell me you want me to fuck you," he said in a husky voice.

"I want you to fuck me."

He stroked faster, stoking the growing fire. "Tell me you want me to come inside you."

I did. I wanted him to fill me and stretch me and make me come as he spilled himself inside me.

"I want you to come inside me," I panted.

I felt his hand press into my tailbone while he slowly fed his dick into me, inch by inch.

"Not like that," I whispered. I was so close already. This was torture.

Slowly, he withdrew and then repeated the excruciatingly slow pace. "I like this," he said, his voice low and gruff. "I like watching you squirm with need while I bury myself inside you."

"Please, no more teasing."

"Then tell me what you want," he said. "Say it like you mean it."

"I want you to fuck me. Hard."

He bowed his body over me, his hand beside mine, gripping the chair. His other hand wrapped around my stomach, and I held my breath, knowing he was in the perfect position to drive deep, just like I asked.

"Do it," I begged.

He slammed into me with one brutal stroke, and my breath hissed from my mouth. Sweet pain and delicious pleasure shot through me as the head of his large shaft bottomed out. I moaned, unable to speak. He felt so good, so real, so—

He thrust again using his strong arm to keep me from moving away. I groaned, wanting more. It was animalistic and sinful being fucked by this man.

He let out a muted grunt from deep inside his chest and pulled out, only to repeat the motion with a ferocious pace. The chair edged forward with the sheer force of his pounding. I whimpered with each stroke. I couldn't take it anymore. I needed to come.

He pulled his chest away from my back and

gripped my hips, changing the angle of his penetration. The moment his velvety head slammed inside me, it ignited a spark. I cried out, feeling that spark turn into an explosion. He quickly reached forward, pressing two thick fingers over my c-spot, stroking it in time to his pistoning hips.

I couldn't speak or breathe or think. The wave hit hard, sucking me in, drowning me in sheer pleasure. I gritted my teeth and dug my nails into the top of the armchair. "Ohmygod. Don't stop. Don't stop."

He didn't. With sharp short jabs of his shaft and the pressure of his fingers, he coaxed every orgasmic contraction from me.

After a long, delicious moment, I felt my mind returning to my body. James returned his strong hands to my hips and to thoughts of his own release.

He began fucking me hard again, showing my body no mercy. I grunted and moaned while he pounded me from behind. I loved it. I loved knowing that he hungered for me like this.

He pushed one last time, and I relished the sensation of his cock pumping his hot cum inside me. I ignited all over again. I reached down and pressed my fingers between my slick folds, coming hard. My walls contracted around his girth, milking every drop.

After several long moments, a gravelly groan escaped his lips, and he leaned into me, his dick still twitching.

"Are you okay?" He planted his forehead between my shoulder blades.

"Yes," I panted, trying to catch my breath. "That was intense."

He withdrew and turned me around, planting a lazy kiss on my mouth before scooping me up. He carried me into my bedroom and laid me down across the bed. I expected him to pass out beside me, but instead he nestled himself between my legs and slid his still-erect cock inside me.

My breath hitched from the unexpected intrusion.

"Am I hurting you?" he asked.

"No. It's a little sensitive right now."

He smiled and began moving his hips slowly. "Then I will be gentle."

"How are you even able to do that?"

"As I said, I have wisdom on my side."

"Am I really the first to experience your *wisdom*?" I asked, completely blown away by his expert skills.

"Yes."

Impressive. And I couldn't lie. It completely turned me on. He'd been waiting all this time for me when he could've had any woman he wanted and simply paid penance.

"How long can you stay…up?" I asked.

"Long enough to make you come again, which helps with…" He cleared his throat but didn't finish his sentence.

Ah. That. He was thinking about me getting pregnant and probably didn't want to spook me by bringing it up again. He knew this was difficult for me.

"You really want to leave something behind," I whispered, brushing my fingertips over his rough cheek.

Instead of answering, he covered my mouth with his and began the task of stoking my arousal once more. By the time he was done, I felt limp and raw and drenched in sweat. Every inch of my body smelled like his sweet scent.

James, having come multiple times, too, lay there with his eyes closed, looking completely spent. We both drifted off. I dreamed of that beach again and of James holding my hand, the warm wind whipping through our hair while we laughed. Somehow, I knew this was my perfect moment. The fantasy I would forever dream of having. Not the walking on the beach, but that feeling in my heart that everything was perfect. We had no worries. Just love and all the time in the world.

When I woke, it was almost seven at night. I turned on the lamp on the nightstand, seeing he'd left me a note.

Sorry to leave you and your beautiful, naked body.

See you tonight at eight for dinner. Wear something sexy.

Love,
James

I showered my sore body, noting that some spots were tenderer than others. I would have to tell that man to take it easy on me.

Who am I kidding? I can't say no to him.

Not having brought a ton of clothes on what was only meant to be a one-week trip, I threw on my little black dress—the one I'd worn the night I met James. I dried my hair and put it into a teased-out top knot to keep my neck cool. A little mascara and red lipstick, and I was ready. I hoped tonight wouldn't be awkward. I hoped the members of James's "private club" didn't hate me for what was happening. I hadn't wished it or even knew about it. Still, I'd been the catalyst. And I wasn't naïve enough to believe that everyone was happy about dying. James himself had said that his aunt was upset.

Well, better suck it up. James wanted me there, and I'd given him my commitment to be with him for however long we had.

When I got to the dinner club, which was really a wide-open room with a thatched roof, all sitting on pillars over the calm water of the small bay, I was surprised by how many people were there. A hundred and fifty? Two hundred? It was a large space and packed from wall to wall.

James's tall, spectacularly built frame stood out among the crowd, even though almost every man on the island looked like a fit athlete or underwear model. Really, I'd never seen so many beautiful people, including the women, who mostly ran the behind-the-scenes operations rather than *played* with the guests.

I wonder how many are in "the club"?

I weaved my way through the crowd, who were all elegantly dressed and sipping champagne. Swing music, piped into the room, gave the event a lively feel. On the surface anyway.

As I skirted past people, some fell silent, and I felt their eyes burning into the back of my head. Others continued chatting away.

Oh boy. This is going to be a rough night.

I came up behind James, who wore a tux and literally made my knees weak.

"Stephanie." Beaming, he took my hands and spread out my arms, drinking me in with his sparkling eyes. "My, my. How stunning you loo…" His words faded off when he got to my pink flip-flops.

"With the bandage and stitches, I couldn't squeeze into my heels."

"You look stunning." He leaned in to whisper in my ear, "But not nearly as gorgeous as the way I left you. Naked. Sated. Pink swollen lips curved up in the corners. What were you dreaming about?"

I batted my eyelashes. "You."

He stood up tall, still holding onto my hands. "Do not look at me like that, Miss Fitzgerald. Not unless you wish me to take you outside and remove that dress." He cracked a smile.

"I might like that. But I think *she* needs a rest." My eyes darted down to my groin.

He laughed with a deep, velvety voice that carried across the room and drew several people's attention. "She will get no such thing." He leaned in. "My cock is already stirring for you. I'm having to think of very unpleasant things simply not to pitch a giant tent right here."

I crinkled my nose. "Please don't. You'd look like a horny penguin and that's an image I can do without."

He chuckled.

"So when are all these people leaving?" I asked.

"The two jets will take the first fifty out tonight. The rest will go in the morning."

I did some quick math. "Only half this room is going?"

He nodded, and I felt the blood drain from my face.

"What is the matter?" he asked.

"Nothing. It's just…I didn't think that so many were part of your *special* team," I whispered that last part.

"You think only the rich clientele deserve a second chance?"

"No. Not at all."

"Good, because I do not either. Many have come here looking for work and stayed once I made them an offer."

"So they had to pay you in work?"

"I asked them to stay for two years to help us, but most stay longer. Or they leave and return. It's become quite the family over the years."

I didn't know what to say. "Are you sure this has to end, James?"

"Yes, my love."

"But did you try?" I pushed.

"I did not have to."

"So you might be wrong. Take a swim. Test it out."

"Stephanie, it is difficult to understand for someone who hasn't done it, but once you've had the *treatment*, you feel it inside you. You feel connected to this place and everyone who's been touched by the waters. I can tell you right now, that as we speak, it is gone. My heart only feels one thing and that is love for you."

I blew out a breath. "Can't you at least try to—"

"Stephanie, you must trust me; there is nothing left for me to do."

I stared up at him. My insides percolated with a silent, growing rage. *This can't be the end. It fucking just can't.*

"Rook!" a deep voice called out.

It was Luke, standing on the stage with a microphone in his hand. "Get up here!"

James took my hand and kissed the top. "It is speech time."

He moved through the crowd, shaking hands, giving hugs and kisses to the women, who all adored him, of course.

Once on stage, Luke and he embraced like brothers. I instantly remembered what James had said about testing me.

Luke was a test. James had wanted to know if I could be tempted by any pretty face. I crossed my arms. I supposed I almost had, but not because I'd wanted Luke more. I'd wanted to cure myself of my real desire for James.

Dirty, dirty monk. I'm going to have to make him pay for that.

Luke left the stage and sidled up to me. "Hey, ex-roomie."

"Shut up. I'm not talking to you, old man."

Luke let loose a throaty laugh. "Why should *you* be mad?"

"You lied to me."

He shrugged. "So I fudged a bit—I said Iraq, when really it was World War II. Sue me."

I shook my head at him.

"Oh, come on, Stephanie." Luke nudged me with his elbow. "Any fool could see you only wanted my uncle."

My head whipped in Luke's direction. *What. The. Fuck?* "Uncle?"

"Didn't he tell you?"

"He only told me that everyone died except for his aunt."

"True. Everyone who came to this island. But Rook's eldest sister, Liliana, had already been married off to a wealthy plantation owner in the Virgin Islands when Rook's father fled with his slave bride."

I frowned and cringed. Why had James not told me?

"Don't look so surprised," said Luke. "Rook wanted nothing to do with my family for many, many years. Then slavery ended, people changed, the plantation was sold to a company, and my great-grandmother was born. She had nothing to do with any of that."

"How did she find Rook?"

"She didn't. He kept tabs on the bloodline. Honestly, I think he was hoping that someday he could establish a new connection with the right person."

"That person was you."

"Yes," Luke replied. "The war fucked me up. My body came home, but my mind stayed trapped in the trenches. Rook found me in a hospital and brought me here. He helped me, gave me another chance."

My eyes teared, and I whisked them away just as James took the mic.

"Good evening, everyone." The room applauded and cheered.

I never would've guessed it from my first icy encounter with James on the island, but these people adored him. Club members or not.

James waved his palms downward to plead for silence. "Thank you. Thank you, all. But as everyone knows, tonight is both a celebration and a sad farewell."

"Boo! Boo!" one guy called out, heckling James jokingly.

Smiling, he shook his head at the man. "Shut that mouth of yours, Adam. Or I'll feed you to the hungry tourists."

Everyone laughed. Even me. I'd seen firsthand how hungry the nonnatives were.

James cleared his throat and straightened his back. The warmth evaporated from his face, and it made my stomach uneasy. Poker face. Which meant whatever he was about to say wasn't easy for him.

Goddammit. I couldn't lie, I wanted James. I wanted to stay with him and be grateful for however many days we had. But standing here in the big room of people who loved him and each other like family, I couldn't feel good about any of this. I couldn't swallow that he had to let go of everything he loved just to have me.

I began to wonder if there wasn't some way to fix all this. Could James retake his vow and give us more time? If he could, would he, or would he hate me for even asking? *Is there a way to slow the aging?*

As James stood on the stage, telling the staff that he wished them prosperity and happiness, I began realizing that he and I didn't have the same definition of love. In his mind, love was acceptance. It was reconciling the good with the bad. His family had died violently right in front of his eyes. And what person wouldn't struggle not to think of that tragedy every time he or she wanted to honor their memory? I know I would. Fuck, I wasn't even able to quietly remember my own mother on her birthday without thinking about how I grew up missing her or how it destroyed my father. The point was, for James, he seemed all too ready to accept that our love had to come with this heart-breaking ending because that was just life.

Well, I'm not ready, I thought to myself. I didn't want to lose one more person. Love was far too precious not to fight for it. Especially when it came to a man like him. He was loyal and devoted to a fault. He was passionate and determined. *He is truly the most incredible man I've ever met.*

Okay, so I'll tell him when he's done with the speech. We'll find a doctor who specializes in the aging process. We'll find the world's most knowledgeable religious historian to ask about the fountain of youth. We'll get on our knees and beg.

The sound of applause pulled me from my thoughts. I'd missed whatever James said, but I noticed the room turning to stare at me, not all of them happy faces.

With wide eyes, I glanced up at James, whose handsome face glowed with a radiant smile, dimples and all.

"Well?" James prodded.

"Uh...I..." I glanced nervously from side to side.

Luke leaned in. "Come on, Stephanie. Say yes."

"Yes to what?" I whispered back out of the side of my mouth.

Luke chuckled. "You really missed all that?"

I snarled with my eyes.

"He asked you to marry him. Here. Now."

"Now, now?" I asked Luke.

"Yes."

I turned my attention back to James, now looking a little impatient and no longer smiling.

Oh boy. I hadn't been expecting this tonight. I wanted to talk to him and agree that we weren't going to let him walk off into the sunset without a fight. Which meant I also needed to tell him about...

Fucking shit. Warner Price.

I'd pushed Warner and the entire horrible mess to the back of my mind for one simple reason: The moment James had told me he only had weeks to live, it no longer mattered. Warner could buy the island, steal it, do whatever he wanted. It meant nothing to me if James was dead. In any case, one quick phone call to Warner to tell him he'd get no fight taking it over would get him to back down and stop threatening my friends and family.

But now, now I intended going another route, which would involve James and me leaving the island and hopefully finding a solution. I couldn't leave the Warner situation on the back burner for two more weeks or not tell James about it. Not when I needed to make sure that my friends didn't end up in a dumpster.

I held up my finger. "I need to talk to you. Outside for a moment."

The room fell into a silence so heavy and thick with awkwardness, you could scoop it up with a spoon.

James's beautiful lips went flat, and his eyes narrowed a bit. "Of course."

I turned and headed outside, feeling my cheeks burn with embarrassment. I hated making a scene, but this discussion had to happen.

I kept walking down the path away from the dinner club, toward the private beach and well out of earshot from anyone inside.

Within seconds, his tall, well-built shadow appeared.

I waited, fidgeting with my hands. *Don't be nervous. He'll understand.* But would he? He might get why I wanted to fight for his life, but would he understand about Warner?

"Please don't tell me you've got cold feet and need time to think about it," James snarled, stopping a foot in front of me. "Because I don't need to point out that time is the one thing I do not have."

"I'm aware of that, yes. And no, I haven't changed my mind about you. Or us," I added and took his strong hand in mine. The light of the dock and building, from where we'd just come, gave off a subtle glow, allowing me to see the displeased expression on his face. It only put me more on edge. I didn't want to hurt him. Not now. Not when we had so little time to act.

"Well?" he said, his voice stern. "What's the problem, then?"

I cleared my throat. "I don't know how to say this, so I'll just spit it out. I can't do what you asked. I can't stay here and watch you die without lifting a finger to stop it."

He dropped my hand and rubbed the back of his neck, groaning with a gravelly voice.

I continued anyway, "Listen. I get that you have it all planned out in your mind—this quiet, peaceful departure with me by your side, lovingly holding your hand. But I can't accept you dying. And I definitely can't let you go without having attempted to fix this."

"Stephanie," he snapped, "there is nothing to fix. The lagoon is dying, and I will die with it."

"So..." my mind spun for a moment, "it still works?"

"It's over, Stephanie. That is all you need to know."

"But did you try it? Did you swim?" I felt like

he wasn't telling me something.

"I do not have to. I already know what is happening. And you should accept what I'm telling you. It's over. The lagoon. My vows. Me. The only thing remaining is us, and I won't poison it by feeding you false hopes."

"But have you ever seen a doctor or had someone test the water? What about researching historical records? Maybe there's a key to how it works and we can—"

"Stephanie," he snapped, "I am no fool. I have done all those things and then some, but it was all a waste of time and money because it only confirmed what I already know. There is no scientific or medical explanation for any of it. Just like there was no explanation for why Father Rook could touch a person and heal them. So you either accept it as truth or you don't. You have faith or you don't."

"Well, I don't accept it. And I don't accept defeat. And I don't accept the part you're asking me to play."

"What are you saying?" he asked. "Are you leaving?"

"No. We are. That's what I'm proposing. If you want to be together, then we have to do it my way. And my way means we see a doctor—five doctors— ten doctors—however many there are in the world who specialize in this kind of stuff and we have to see—"

"So you propose I spend the final weeks of my

life away from the only place that has given me peace. The place my family is buried and—"

"If you really want to be with me, then *you* have to accept that I couldn't live with myself or let you go without doing everything possible to try to save you first." I whisked away the tears from under my eyes. "If I don't, then I'll never know and it will haunt me for the rest of my life. And if you really care about me, you wouldn't want that."

James rubbed his thick stubble, sighing toward the sandy ground. "I should've known you would not be content to do things my way. You don't give up easily."

"I don't give up on the people I love," I said.

James was silent for several long moments. "I will think it over, and you'll have my answer in the morning." He stepped in close and slid his warm hand to the nape of my neck. "But I'll do my thinking after I've had you in my bed tonight."

The desirous effect was instant, only now it felt stronger than ever, reaching far beyond the simple definition of lust. I needed him with every ounce of my soul. I wanted him with everything I had.

"You can have me as many times as you want," I said. "Just promise to think it over seriously. This isn't just about you. Not if we're together and I have to try to go on without you."

He bowed his head and placed a soft kiss on my lips. "I promise. And now that you've spoken your mind, I must return to our guests and inform them that there will be no wedding before the party ends tonight."

"I'm sorry. I really am." I wanted to vow to love, cherish, and care for him until "death do us part," but it would be a lie. I needed to be honest with myself and him. I could only live through the pain of losing him if I knew we'd exhausted all hope. But sitting back and watching him wither? No. I wouldn't recover from that even if I lived two or three lifetimes like he had.

"It is fine, Stephanie," he said. "We would've had to make the ceremony very short anyway. The first plane departs in thirty minutes."

"So soon?"

"We have much to do and little time. Best to clear the island quickly of anyone who might cause you problems later on."

I supposed if half the staff noticed some of the other half aging rapidly, it would raise eyebrows. James didn't want anyone asking questions or drawing the wrong sort of attention from outsiders.

He kissed me again. "Thank you for your honesty. At least we have that between us." He turned and headed back to the party.

Meanwhile, my stomach suddenly felt like it had a cold, heavy bowling ball rolling around inside it.

I didn't tell him about Warner. Shit. Shit. Shit. But other than wanting to selfishly clear my own conscience, what was the point? If James decided to stick to his guns, it would all be over soon. And I didn't want him living his last days worrying about Warner Price or feeling like I'd stabbed him in the back. The situation wasn't so black and white. I'd had my reasons, even if I now regretted them. But how was I to know that I would fall in love with the infamous Mr. Rook? No. I would wait. If James and I left the island, then I'd tell him and hope he understood that I'd acted with Warner out of desperation. Then, hopefully, James knew enough powerful people to deal with Warner. He couldn't be the first gangster to want the island.

I began walking in the direction of the party, but found myself reluctant to face James.

Goddammit, what's the matter with me? Who was I kidding? I had to tell him about Warner. I had to have faith that we would find a way to save James, and how would he feel knowing I'd kept such a huge horrible secret?

Now was the time. He'd had his secrets and come clean. I had to do the same.

"He lied to you, you know," said a voice, female with a slight accent.

I turned my head to find James's aunt stepping from the shadows.

"I thought you left." I placed my hand over my heart.

"I returned on the plane this morning."

"Does Rook know?" I asked.

"You think I do not have friends here, willing to

keep my secrets? You think everyone follows James blindly and wants to walk with him to the grave?" Her French-Caribbean accent came through clearly.

"I already know about the lagoon," I said. "I can't tell you how sorry I am. I can't imagine how hard this must be on you—"

"She did not drown. Not like you think," she said.

My entire body solidified into stone. "Sorry?"

"That lagoon is cursed," she hissed, her voice barely above a whisper. "It demands blood."

"What are you talking about?" I felt my heart squeeze painfully inside my chest.

She grabbed me by the shoulders, speaking in an ominous voice. "Father Rook died with a curse on his lips. His soul will not rest until things are made right."

"Rest how? And what does this have to do with Cici?"

"Whateva happened to Father Rook when he died, the rage he felt for what those men did to us, what he watched them do to me and the child I carried, it leeched into that water. It heals, just as he did, but it demands blood, too."

"What kind of blood?"

"The blood of those men who raped me, who killed his child." She leaned in. "Your sister's blood. *Your* blood."

She's insane. "I have to go see James." I pulled away from her.

"Your great-great-grandfather was on that ship."

What the fuck? "The ship that sank?"

"Thirty-seven washed onto our shores. But there were over ninety in that crew, and many survived on small boats or swam to other islands."

The blood drained from my limbs and rushed to my heart and lungs. "You must be mistaken. James wouldn't keep that from me. He wouldn't..." I was about to say that he wouldn't lie, but I already knew he would. *No. No. Not like this. He wouldn't do this to me.*

"We ran out of blood, Stephanie, a long time ago. The men we have left never came ashore during the massacre. They never touched me or my family or Father Rook's brothers. They are useless."

"I don't believe you." This couldn't be right.

"It does not matta what you believe," she spat with her thick accent. "James led your sister to that water. He has led hundreds upon hundreds more."

As she spoke, my mind began picking away at all of the little things I'd managed to ignore or dismiss to conveniently justify what my heart desired. The saliva tests. James's insistence that I not go near that water. The dreams I'd had of the monk beckoning me to follow him to the water, and of Cici crying out to me.

No. It can't be true. Because if it was, it meant I'd fallen in love with the man who murdered my sister, that I had once again fallen for his lies, like some fool who was so broken and lost that she'd believe anything.

"Why are you telling me all this?" I demanded.

"Because I am not like James. I keep my vows, and I will make things right." She reached for my arm, and in an instant, I knew what she meant to do.

I wasn't going to end up like Cici.

I swung as hard as I could with my right fist, landing a blow on the side of her face. She grunted on impact and whirled back, falling to the ground.

I turned and ran for the trees, my mind racing, my stitches ripping open with each stride. I winced, but the pain was no match for my adrenaline.

Where do I go? Where do I go? Back to the party filled with her friends? Or back to James, the man who murdered my sister? The man who, at every step of the way, had systematically and meticulously fed me lie after lie and had manipulated me, fucked me, and asked me to love him until the bitter end.

Why would you do that to me, Rook? I couldn't breathe. And I had nowhere to go.

Not true. I headed for the landing strip, one flip-flop slick with blood. I made it to the tree line beside the runway and then stopped. The small jet was there, lights on, people climbing the steps to board.

If I got on the plane, Rook would know. Some-one would tell him. *Or her.*

Panicked and sick with rage, I took a breath.

No. The passengers getting on that plane

weren't part of their little fucking demented club. They were the regular staff, the only exception maybe being the pilots.

I looked toward the cockpit and saw two people inside. Okay. If I hurried, I could board without them seeing me.

I glanced over my shoulder, praying that Rook's aunt wouldn't catch me. Then again, what would she do? Cause a scene in front of so many witnesses?

I didn't know, but I had to risk it.

Calmly, I walked toward the plane and the line of people.

"Stephanie, coming to see us off?"

Holy shit. No, fuck no. It was Julie. She had been my personal concierge three weeks ago, and I had treated her like absolute shit. I mean, I literally gave her hell. But I had been told that the infamous Mr. Rook didn't mingle with the riffraff, and I'd been determined to get his attention any way possible. That meant playing the part of disgruntled guest. To my detriment, it had worked, but that wouldn't win me any points with this woman.

She smiled. "Or are you escaping our esteemed employer and his wedding proposal." She leaned in with a sadistic grin. "Did he turn out to be more than you could handle?"

Hell of hells. Of course. She'd been at the party. She'd witnessed the entire debacle. I had to decide quickly—make up some lie or plead for her help.

"Julie, you have no reason to believe me when I

say this, but I am not a bad person. I have never treated anyone like I treated you."

"Lucky me to be the first." She grinned with a bitchy smirk.

I grabbed her arm. "Well, I'm sorry. I had to do it, and I can't tell you why or how sorry I am. But now I need to get on this plane. They can't know," I whispered.

She eyed me for a long moment. "I could lose my termination package for that."

"Please, I'm begging you; just don't call attention to me. If they find me, they do, but don't let it be on your conscience."

With hesitation, she gave me a nod and then turned toward the plane. When it was her turn to board, I followed as closely as I could, hoping to blend in and that her body might shield my face a bit.

As carefully as possible, I walked behind her, forcing myself not to cry from the pain or walk funny. The rowdy passengers, all coming from the party, seemed distracted and drunk. Julie went to the back of the plane, and I slid into the bathroom. I hadn't gone unseen, but no one seemed to think twice about me being on the plane. People came and went all the time. *Except the ones Rook murders.*

With the door locked, I held my breath and waited for the roar of the engines. It didn't take long.

"Roll call!" I heard a deep voice call over the

intercom.

Oh shit. Oh shit. At first, I didn't hear anything, but as the pilot made his way down the aisle, the people calling out their names became clearer.

"And you are?" said the captain's voice.

"Julie Eidelman."

Please don't rat me out. Please don't rat me out. I pressed my ear to the door, expecting to be dragged out of the bathroom at any moment. I deserved it in Julie's eyes.

"All right, Mike! All cleared for takeoff."

I let out a sigh of relief. Within minutes, we were in the air. Once I heard voices rumbling in the galley, people laughing and mixing drinks, I slipped out and found a quiet seat next to Julie.

"Thank you," I said.

"Don't mention it."

CHAPTER EIGHTEEN

The rest of the flight back to the small private airport south of Newark had me on pins and needles. The entire time, I expected the pilot to turn around and take me back. When we finally landed, the passengers beyond sloshed, no one was happier than me to feel the gust of cold New Jersey air.

One by one, we shuffled out, me with paper towels wedged between my blood-crusted foot and stained flip-flop.

Julie didn't say a word the remainder of the flight or bother looking at me when we passed the cockpit.

"Goodbye. It's been a pleasure." The pilot doled out the polite nods. "Take care. Be sure to take a cab, Barb," he said to the woman staggering out in front of Julie.

"Aye-aye, captain!" Barb replied.

When it was my turn to pass the captain, his face turned a pale shade of taupe. Our eyes met, and I knew he recognized me.

What can he do now? I was surrounded by non-club members, and I would fight tooth and nail if he so much as laid a hand on me.

I leaned toward him as I passed by. "I don't think they'll reward you for setting me free, but I won't tell if you don't."

The captain's face turned red with anger, but he looked away toward the staggering stragglers behind me.

I limped down the steel staircase and looked up at the sky. *I made it. I fucking made it.* Only now I'd have to contend with the painful fact that this wasn't over.

Mr. Rook killed my Cici. He murdered her. And for all I knew, they'd planned to do the same to me after he'd had his own fantasy fun.

In either case, it wouldn't take long for them to find me. I had to act quickly.

I got into a cab and told the driver to take me home. "That's a two-and-a-half-hour ride home, lady."

I didn't have a purse, wallet or cell phone. But I had an emergency credit card at home in my dresser. I could pay him with that. "How fast can you drive?"

Exhausted and emotionally broken, I returned to the home I had once shared with Cici. The slower than expected three-hour drive, due to an accident in the road, had given me clarity, but not a solution.

Rook had to pay for what he'd done. I didn't care why he'd lied or to what end. All that mattered was that Cici got her justice.

Of course, I felt enraged and heartbroken over having fallen for Rook's slick lies, but I refused to feel like a fool for who I was. *I'm done with that.* I was done ridiculing myself for believing in love or being the person who dared to risk it all for a chance of having it.

So I loved too much?

So I cared too deeply?

So the fuck what! That didn't make me weak or worthless. It made people like Rook monsters and nothing more. This very morning, I would go see Warner and tell him what I'd found. Rook and his aunt would get what they deserved not because I was vengeful, but because I wanted to live, and I deserved to.

Standing in our old yellow kitchen, I looked down at my foot. The paper towel I'd taped on had saturated with blood and was dripping all over the old brown and white linoleum. *Dammit.* I needed to get to the ER. My dad's car, an old beige Volvo, was parked in the driveway. He always left it for us when he traveled, which was pretty much all the time.

I glanced at the clock hanging on the wall above Cici's kitten calendar. Her kindergarten class had given it to her last Christmas, and it still displayed June—the month my world came crashing down.

I walked over and changed the page to October.

I had to move forward now—if not for her, then for my own sake.

Okay. It's almost seven thirty in the morning. I could get my foot mended and then head into the city to see Warner.

A loud knock at the front door startled me down to the marrow in my bones.

Wait. It couldn't be James or his aunt. They were four hours away by plane, plus the drive time. *Unless he figured out I left and followed.* He said they had two jets.

I hesitated, thinking about running, until I spotted a shadowy figure at the back door, which was next to the side carport.

"Stephanie!"

Warner. Fucking Warner. I covered my face with my hands and blew out. How did he know I was here?

What does it matter? I wanted to see him anyway.

I jerked open the back door, finding Warner Price not dressed in a suit, but in a black long-sleeved shirt and black pants. A black baseball hat covered his short dark hair.

"Mr. Price, how nice of you to stop by. I just got back and planned to see you this morn—"

He reached his large hand through the doorway, grabbing a fistful of my hair. "You think you can just take my money and blow me off, you little cunt?"

"I didn't! I didn't blow you off!" I screamed as he dragged me outside. Somewhere, in the recess of my mind, I knew there were more men with him. Someone was lifting my legs while he dragged me to the trunk of his car and then threw me in.

"Please," I pleaded for my life, "I didn't fuck you over. I didn't. I promise I got what you needed."

Warner Price looked down at me with those unkind eyes. "The only thing I need is you at the bottom of the ocean."

The trunk slammed shut, sealing me in complete darkness.

TO BE CONTINUED...

But keep reading for a short story and clues about CHECK, coming 2018.

www.mimijean.net/check.html

Or sign up for new release alerts.

https://goo.gl/9NZiqR

WILMA SALINGER

Despite Mr. Rook's efforts to prepare me, it had been nothing like I'd expected. *Far more frightening.* Though, had I known, I might not have gone through with it. Getting into that lagoon, facing the unknown, had given me a genuine heart attack. If it hadn't been for Mr. Rook coming to hold me under the water, I would have kicked the bucket right then and there.

I looked in the bathroom mirror for the fiftieth time this morning. My skin was so soft and smooth. My light green eyes were vibrant. And when I flexed the hands once riddled with arthritis, they felt strong and young again. Not the hands of an eighty-year-old.

Wilma, I told myself, *you should be outside, looking at the view, walking on the beach.* With sunscreen, of course. Lots of sunscreen. I never wore it the first time around, but I would now. *Not taking any chances.*

In my colorful one-piece bathing suit and pair of long red shorts, I went out to my balcony overlooking Miami Beach. The balmy wind gusted across my face almost like it wanted to welcome me to my new life.

I heard the front door slam shut.

"Hey! You ready to go, honey?" called a familiar female voice. "I got ice, beer, and sandwiches."

It was my new roommate, Meg. Meg Purdue. We'd met on the plane ride home from Rook's Island and hit it off immediately.

Full of redhead spunk, that one. Though on the outside she was twice my age—in her forties. She'd recently left her wealthy cheating husband, and with her daughter grown and off to college, she and I got to talking, sparking all kinds of ideas. "I've always wanted to live somewhere warm, just like Mr. Rook's Island," I'd said on the plane, my head still buzzing with the effects of the lagoon.

"Me too!" Meg had said while guzzling martinis from her seat next to me.

"Then let's do it. I've got money." My Bob had worked hard and saved carefully, leaving me a tidy sum. Of course, I gave most of it to my kids—who I missed more than anything—but I'd kept a few million for myself. A good start to a new life.

Anyway, it had turned out that Meg had millions in the bank as part of her divorce settlement, and she planned on living the rest of her life as a free woman in the pursuit of happiness.

My kind of gal!

"I'm out here!" I called to Meg, still shocked by the sound of my twenty-year-old voice. "Just grabbing my things for the beach."

"Oh no. Please don't tell me you're going in

that." Meg shook her head at me from the open sliding glass door.

I looked down at my outfit. "What's the matter with this, dear?"

"You dress like an eighty-year-old woman, that's what's the matter."

I tried not to smile.

She added, "If I had a body like yours, I'd be showin' it off every chance I got! Look at those perky boobs."

"Well, I-I…" I was still a product of my time. Women born in the 1930s just didn't run around with their rears blowing in the wind unless they intended to sell it.

"Come on." Meg waved at me. "I'm taking you shopping for a real bathing suit, one that's worthy of Miami Beach."

I gave her a hesitant look. Meg liked spandex, animal prints, and anything shiny.

"You're beautiful, Jenny. What do you have to hide?"

That my name isn't Jenny?

Oddly, it turned out that Jenny wasn't just my new name, but also the name of Meg's daughter. I wasn't sure if Rook had planned it that way, but it had certainly helped the two of us bond immediately. The other Jenny was currently in New York, getting ready to attend some big fashion school. Meg wouldn't shut up about it, but I understood. I'd raised my own two daughters.

"Thank you, Meg. And I accept your offer of

shopping, but I won't be wearing any of those strings up my rear. I want fabric. I'm a lady."

She laughed. "You're a strange one is what you are. Come on."

I stepped inside, locked the sliding door, and went for my sandals by the sofa right as the phone rang. "Got it." I grabbed the thing from the end table and fiddled with the buttons. I could see now—clear as day—but I still needed to get accustomed to all these newfangled contraptions I'd never had at home. Bob never spent a dime on anything new.

"Hello?" I answered.

"Wilma, is that you?" said the voice on the other end. My heart did the fox-trot. That wasn't my name anymore. And I hadn't told anyone from my past life where I was. Except for Marjorie, my good friend. She'd been the one to tell me about Mr. Rook's fountain of youth after she'd heard I was dying of lung cancer, thanks to years of breathing in all that tar from Bob's damned cigarettes.

"Yes," I replied. "This is Jenny." I looked at Meg and gave her the one-second hand signal.

"Wilma." Marj sounded panicked. "Have you heard from Rook?"

"Uh, no. Can't say I have."

"Something's wrong, Wilma. Something's terribly wrong." She panted.

"Where are you? What's the matter?"

"I'm at home. I-I don't know what's happening."

I stood from the sofa and took the cordless phone into my bedroom, closing the door behind me. "What do you mean?" I whispered.

"I'm aging."

"Calm yourself, Marj. Mr. Rook told us that we would. You can't stay young forever."

"I know. I know. But when I woke up this morning, I looked different. Like I've aged ten years."

My guts did a nasty old summersault. "Did you call Mr. Rook?"

"He's not answering." She began to sob. "What do I do?"

"I don't know. But...stay calm. I'll call you back." I hung up and went for my nightstand to grab the card Mr. Rook had given me. *Call day or night. I'm always here for you,* he'd said.

I dialed the eight-hundred number and it rang twenty times. No one answered. I tried three more times without luck.

"Jenny!" Meg knocked on my bedroom door. "What are you doing in there? Let's go, girl. The beach awaits!"

"Be right there, I forgot to...trim something." I winced at my ridiculous excuse and set the phone down on my dresser.

Saint Joseph. I gasped, catching a glimpse of myself in the mirror. I had a liver spot on my cheek.

TO BE CONTINUED...

www.mimijean.net/check.html

AUTHOR'S NOTE

Hello, my lovely VIPs!

Who's ready for another swim? Because there's at least one book left in this chapter of Mr. Rook's story, and I sense a major cluster fuck on the horizon. Not only that, but it seems Stephanie wasn't the only person who got a surprise ending.

Do you think Rook knew about Wilma and the other guests' premature aging? I don't. If anything, they'll all be forced to make some ugly choices if they want to survive Warner Price. I can't wait to see what happens!

As soon as I get through…through…whoa, what's the name of the book? I can't remember. Totally *forgot*! (Wink, wink.) In any case, once I'm through with *that* book and SKINNY PANTS, I will tackle CHECK (Book #3 of Mr. Rook's Island). Be sure to sign up for new release alerts and the random weird crap in my newsletters: https://goo.gl/9NZiqR

As for SWAG, you know what to do! Send an email to mimi@mimijean.net with your full name and shipping address (international okay). If you LURRRVVED the book, be sure to mention if you showed the book-love and wrote a review so I can thank you! I might include extra goodies (usually fridge magnets) as an offering of said book-love, though everything is on a first-come basis! Either way, you'll hear from me personally and get a perrrty-perrrty envelope shipped right from my home in AZ.

For my friends who love my story breakdowns, I beg your forgiveness. One more book, and I'll lay it on you! In the meantime, feel free to listen to the hints in my soundtrack and obsess on "Hooked on a Feeling."

PLAY LIST

open.spotify.com/user/mimijeanpamfiloff/playlist/7naUJSs6ijmtQySRmSok22

WITH EVIL ISLAND LOVE,
Mimi

ACKNOWLEDGMENTS

A special, heartfelt thanks to the pieces on my chessboard who are always there, rooting for my wins!

Javi, Seb, Stef, Nana, Carport, Cass, Rita, Lee, Gary, Gene, Irene, Sash, and Bruce. No matter where I go, family is always my home.

To the amazing Dali, wow! I don't know how you do it AND put up with me. But I'm so glad that you do.

Kylie, thanks for always being a sounding board of reason. I think I'd forget that I'm a writer if you weren't there to remind me.

Ally, you're crazy. Please don't ever stop! I just love it.

Latoya, just in case I've never told you, you're a great editor, but more importantly, you're a fucking inspiration. Go get 'em, woman!

Pauline, how is it possible you don't send me hate mail? After all these years, I still can't use an em dash, ellipses…or-hyphen-correctly.

Paul, thanks for ensuring my books don't get lost in bad formatting, so my readers can get lost in the story and not missing sentences.

With Love,
Mimi, author of 29 books and counting...

2018 RELEASES
THE GODDESS OF FORGETFULNESS

She's spent her whole life hoping to be remembered.

Until him…

www.mimijean.net/forgetty.html

SKINNY PANTS
BOOK 4, THE HAPPY PANTS SERIES

He's the doctor of her dreams.

She's got room to lose.

But this plump ER nurse will have to face facts:

A solid relationship begins when you're ready to take it all off.

www.mimijean.net/skinny-pants.html

DIGGING A HOLE

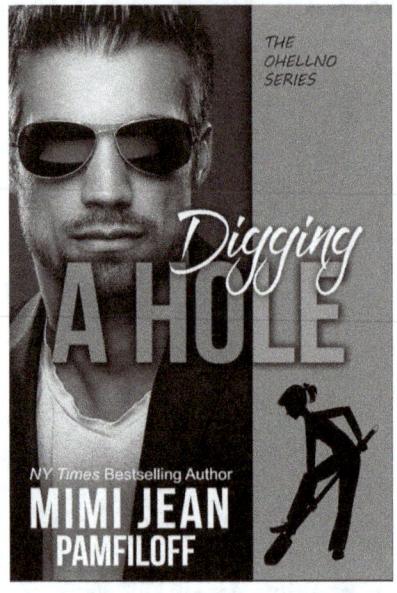

THE OHELLNO SERIES

Digging
A HOLE

NY Times Bestselling Author
MIMI JEAN
PAMFILOFF

He's the meanest boss ever.
She's the sweet shy intern.
They're about to wreck each other crazy.

My name is Sydney Lucas. I am smart, deathly shy, and one hundred percent determined to make my own way in the world. Which is why I jumped at the chance to intern for Mr. Nick Brooks despite his reputation. After ten failed interviews at other companies, he was the only one offering. Plus, everyone says he knows his stuff, and surely a man as stunningly handsome as him can't be "the devil incarnate," right? Wrong.

Oh...that man. That freakin' man has got to go! I've been on the job one week, and he's insulted my mother, wardrobe shamed me, and managed to make me cry. Twice. Underneath that stone-cold, beautiful face is the evilest human being ever.

But I'm not going to quit. Oh no. For once in my life, I've got to make a stand. Only, every time I open my mouth, I can't quite seem to muster the courage. Perhaps my revenge needs to come in another form: destroying him quietly.

Because I've got a secret. I'm not really just an intern, and Sydney Lucas isn't my real name.

FOR EXTRAS, BUY LINKS, and MORE, GO TO:

www.mimijean.net/diggingahole.html

ABOUT THE AUTHOR

San Francisco native MIMI JEAN PAMFILOFF is a *New York Times* bestselling romance author. Although she obtained her MBA and worked for more than fifteen years in the corporate world, she believes that it's never too late to come out of the romance closet and follow your dream. Mimi lives with her Latin lover hubby, two pirates-in-training (their boys), and the rat terrier duo, Snowflake and Mini Me, in Arizona. She hopes to make you laugh when you need it most and continues to pray daily that leather pants will make a big comeback for men.

Sign up for Mimi's mailing list for giveaways and new release news!